IN LOVE WITH A SOUTHERN SAVAGE

BRII TAYLOR
SHANAH LITTLE

TEXT UCP TO 22828 TO SUBSCRIBE TO OUR MAILING LIST

If you would like to join our team, submit the first 3-4 chapters of your completed manuscript to
Submissions@UrbanChapterspublications.com

ONE

Andrea

I wanted to turn over and disable my blaring alarm clock this morning so I could go back to sleep but unfortunately, I couldn't. It was time for my ass to get up and go to AT&T's call center where I've worked for almost two years now. My cousin Aniya got me plugged in because she'd been working there for five years.

I didn't see how she hung in this long. I hated answering phones and dealing with rude ass customers about their phone bills and shit. A couple times I had to curse their asses out because they had me fucked up. It wasn't my fault their lines were disconnected because their broke asses couldn't pay their bills on time.

I never paid any of my bills. Any guy that I was messing with made sure all my shit was paid or I'd go in their pockets when they were sleep and take how much I wanted. These days you had to take what you wanted from these selfish ass men because they thought you were supposed to give up your goods without getting anything in return. Hell naw! If they didn't give me what I wanted, I'd just rob their ass blind like a thief in the night. I wouldn't call myself a hoe because most men I dealt with I'd known for a while, and they just threw money my way because they had it.

Men loved to lay up with my fine ass. My smooth, caramel skin covered my thick frame and small boobs. I was really versatile when it came to my hairstyles. Today I was rocking my short, curly hair because I had a date with my sugar daddy last night and he liked when I looked natural. I usually did little dates and one-night stands with old men I met at the bars when one of my main niggas were acting broke. The old ones were the ones that tried to get over on you, but I was smarter than that.

Recently I learned to slow down on depending on these dudes to give me money. They be so quick to play broke it ain't even funny. That's why I've been trying my best not to leave my petty ass job. And also my aunt rarely let men come in her house. I use to do a lot of cars cracking and scheming but the last time I got locked up my aunt said she wasn't bailing me out again. And jail is a scary ass place. A place you never want to end up for a long period of time.

"Andrea, come on! Get yourself ready before I leave you here." Ugh, my cousin, Aniya, was such a bitch sometimes. She acted like we couldn't be late for work at least one damn day. *She just has to do everything right.*

"Girl, I'm coming, damn. Can a bitch have time to get dressed?"

"A bitch knows when we leave so a bitch should be ready. Fuck!" I laughed because she always says the word *fuck* when she was trying to get smart. Like that shit was going to make me move any faster.

I swung my bedroom door open and walked to the front door where she was standing, waiting for me. We lived in a three-bedroom apartment in Decatur, Georgia with my aunt Anita. Being twenty-five and living with my aunt and cousin wasn't really where I wanted to be, but I was saving up so I could get my own one-bedroom apartment.

Don't get me wrong, I love my aunt and cousin. They took me in after my mom overdosed on drugs. I never knew my dad, and my mother never even mentioned him when I was younger. My aunt really took care of me before my mom passed. My mom and aunt were real close sisters, and my aunt always tried to help my mom get clean. Too bad everything she tried never worked.

Anytime we would put her in a rehab she would run away and not show up for months. She died when I was seventeen. I felt bad because I didn't cry much when she passed. Maybe because I didn't really know her. She was always high and asking me for my damn allowance my aunt gave us every week. Like a dummy, I always gave it to her.

My aunt always yelled and got upset with me when I did that. She always said that I was helping her kill herself. Hell, I just wanted her to get out my face with that begging shit. I just gave her the money so she could go away.

"If you make us late, I'm gonna kill you, girl."

"Get your panties out your ass, girl. We gonna be on time." Aniya unlocked the doors to her 2017 Malibu Chevy and we hopped in.

Aniya was so happy when she first got her car. Hell, I was happy too because I was tired of taking Ubers and the bus to work. To people with money, this car wasn't nothing. But to people like us, in the hood? This car was everything—literally. To see a young chick riding in a 2017 Malibu Chevy meant they had a little money, and bitches envied chicks that had their own car, a job, and money.

Aniya was a supervisor at AT&T, so she made way more money than I did and she could afford the small things she wanted. I would be able to afford them as well with the money I got from my men, but my ass always ended up in the mall, buying shit I didn't even need. It was cool though because I loved riding around with my cousin. She was a couple years older than me so she tries to keep me level and give me advice. Sometimes I listen and sometimes I don't.

"So, what you doing this weekend? We should go out to a club or something. Yo' old lady ass ain't been out the crib in I don't know how long."

I wanted Aniya's boring ass to step out with me because she

never went any-damn-where. She sat in the house every weekend and drank wine with her mom while they watched ratchet reality shows. Don't get me wrong, I loved reality shows, but I wasn't about to sit in the house every weekend watching them.

"Girl, *Love and Hip Hop Atlanta* just started back this Monday and I need to catch up."

"Bitch, is you serious right now?"

"What?"

"We going out this weekend, and I don't want to hear shit else about it. Yo' ass can watch that show Sunday. Sunday is chill day."

"Girl, it depends on where because you know I don't like going to clubs." Aniya began to pop her damn gum. I hated when she did that. The shit was irritating.

"Ok, girl. I will find something for us to do. No clubs, I promise." We pulled into AT&T's parking lot and I instantly became stressed. I literally hated this job. If I could quit, I definitely would, but we help my aunt pay rent and bills and I couldn't depend on the money I get from my little boy toys.

"Girl, you need to stop looking like that. And don't go in here acting a fool today. I can't keep saving your damn job. I'm a supervisor, not God, honey." We laughed and got out of the car. I took a deep breath and collected my thoughts while walking to my cubicle.

"Lord, I will not cuss anyone out today. In the name of Jesus, amen."

"Girl, you funny as hell." My coworker, Brandy, said. She sat in the cubicle next to me every day. I hated when she talked to me. Little did she know, I didn't like her talkative ass like that. She ran around here telling everybody's business but her own. I stayed cordial because the bitch hadn't told any of my business yet.

As soon as I logged into my computer, customers started calling the phone. Like, damn, can a bitch sit down first? I cut the ringer off on my work phone until I was done setting up my area. They had me fucked up if they thought I was going to come in and instantly start talking to customers. I needed to get myself together first.

When I was all settled, I cut the phone back on and took my first call.

"AT&T customer service, how may I assist you today?"

"I paid my damn bill and my phone is still not in service. That's how you can assist me."

"Miss, was your phone out of service when you paid the bill?"

"Ummm, duh, that's why the hell I paid it. Damn, I swear they have the dumbest bitches answering these phones!"

"Excuse me, miss? I didn't hear you. Can you repeat that please?"

"I said they have stupid bitches answering the damn phones!"

"First of all, bitch, if you would have paid your bill on time, then your damn services wouldn't have been cut the hell off. And if you listened to the automated service, it tells you that you need to power cycle your device after paying your bill if your services have been disconnected. Yo' dumb ass wouldn't need to speak to an agent then, would you?"

"Excuse you?" The bitch had the nerve to say like she didn't hear what the fuck I said.

"Bitch, you heard me!"

"Andrea to the office. Now!" My baldheaded ass boss Ben was standing behind me the whole time. I stood up and followed his shiny head to his office.

"Ben, I know what you're gonna say, but that bitch on the phone was rude to me first. Listen to the conversation on the tape." He played the tape back and shook his head.

"No matter what customers say to you, Andrea, they are always right."

"How the hell was she right when she in the wrong?"

"Andrea, this is the third time you've done this."

"Ok and?"

"And that means we gotta let you go."

"Uh, go back to my desk? Aight, big dawg. Thanks for understanding." I stood up and tapped him on the shoulder then walked out his office.

"Andrea, are you serious right now?" Ben asked while I was walking away.

"Hold on, Mr. Ben, my phone ringing at the desk. I got another customer." I looked back and saw him shaking his head and laughed. His ass couldn't fire me. I would sue his ass for sexual harassment because his old ass always flirted with me.

"What the hell you do now, Drea?" Aniya stepped out of her office and asked me.

"Nothing, girl, everything's under control. Mr. Ben's ass trying to act all crazy because I just cussed this old bitch out on the phone."

"Really, Drea?"

"What? She called me a dumb, stupid bitch because her ass ain't pay her bill on time." She shook her head and walked off. I went back to my desk and sat down because he got me fucked up if he thought I was going anywhere.

"Girl, yo' ass on thin ice around here," Brandy said while shaking her head.

"Girl, mind yo' damn business! Always sticking yo' fat ass nose where it don't belong." She looked at me like she was shocked. *Bitch, yes, your nose is big as hell.* I laughed to myself because I knew I wasn't shit.

I skipped out of the office building happy as I could be because it was lunch time. We always went out for lunch because we got an hour break.

"What we about to eat, girl? I hope we not about to go to the chicken and waffles place again because I'm tired of that." We ate at that place so much my ass was going to start clucking. Aniya's ass was so concerned about coming back to work before break was over she didn't want to drive anywhere else. The chicken and waffles place was right around the corner from our job.

"We can go to the BBQ rib shack. I got a taste for some ribs."

"Anything is better than chicken and waffles."

"Girl, shut up. If you get a damn car, you can drive wherever the hell you like."

"Ohhhh, the shade is real up in here, hunny." We laughed as she pulled off in the direction of the restaurant. Luckily, the restaurant was only ten minutes away from the job.

"Damn, how long we been standing in this line? Why the hell is this place so crowded?" I was getting irritated as hell standing in this hot ass restaurant's line for some ribs.

"Why you gotta be so loud in these people restaurant?" Aniya asked while taking her credit card out her wallet.

"Big baller when did get a Discover credit card. Lil' baby out here making major moves. I see you, I see you."

"Girl, you need to cut it out." Aniya laughed as we walked up to the counter. She ordered ribs for the both of us and paid for my food as well. This was why I loved my cousin. Even though I had money, she had more and wasn't selfish with it. We sat down and ate our lunch while having girl talk. I turned around and looked out the restaurant window because someone was outside banging their loud ass music.

"Girl, look at all them dudes out there all loud and shit. Come on, let's go before these fools start acting crazy," Aniya said while packing her food to go.

"Girl, you so damn crazy. They ass ain't thinking about you. Besides, some of them fine as hell." I was looking at one guy in particular that hopped out of the driver's side of the Range Rover. He was fine as hell, and the other guys crowded around him like he a boss or something. We stood to leave the restaurant and I caught him looking at me through the window. When we walked out of the restaurant, all eyes were on us though we were dressed in white button up blouses and black slacks.

"Aye, lil' mama, hold up." I heard Mr. Range Rover yell to me. I kept walking because I didn't want to seem as thirsty as I really was.

"Aye, girl! I know you hear me talking to you!" He caught up to me and grabbed my arm. I snatched away and pulled my pepper spray out.

"Boy, don't put yo' hands on me." I held the mace up to his face but I didn't spray it. He just stood there unbothered like I wouldn't burn his face off.

"Calm yo' ass down. girl. I'm just tryna holler at you for a second."

"Andrea, get in the car," Aniya's scary ass yelled.

"And was is it that you want to holler at me about?"

"You real beautiful and I was wondering if I could take you out sometimes." *Damn, he fine as hell and he smells good too.* He was about five feet seven with waves on swim right now and brown skin that looked like a Reese's Cup. His body was tatted up which made him look thuggish and sexier. *Damn, I just want to take a bite of him right now.* His smile was big and bright, and it looked like he took real good care of his teeth. Rocking basketball shorts and a white tee, I figured he must've just finished playing ball or something.

"You're a complete stranger, boy. I don't know you."

"Well how about you bring your friend along too?"

"Umm, hell no. I think the fuck not. Let's go, Andrea." I turned around to give her that shut the fuck up look, and she shook her head and got in the car.

"Well how about this. You can come to this little backyard party me and my peoples having this Saturday." He gave me a flyer and walked off.

"Bring yo' rude ass friend too. My homies like rude girls." I laughed and hopped in the car.

"Girl, you ain't gonna get enough of talking to strangers."

"He invited us to a backyard party. Look at the flyer."

"I'm not going to this thug ass event."

"Girl, this is gonna be cool. They giving out toys and shit to the kids. It's gonna be food and drinks. Take the stick out yo' ass for one day. Why you gotta act all bougie? Bitch, we grew up in the same house and I don't act as bougie as you do."

"I'm not acting bougie, I just want to be in a safe place. Those dudes back there looked rough as hell."

"Girl, we going."

"I'll think about it, Drea." I clapped my hands and danced in my seat because every time Aniya said she'd think about that meant yes. *Mr. Range Rover gonna be my new sponsor.*

TWO

Aniya

I wanted to be anywhere but at this damn backyard party with Drea. A deal was a deal though. She said if she could get through the rest of the week without going off on somebody at work I had to come to this party. If she didn't, I could stay home with my mama to watch my shows and sip wine "with my old ass". Her words, not mine.

I know it was wrong to say, but I honestly didn't think she'd make it. If you knew my cousin, you'd feel the same way.

Drea has always been the more outgoing of the two of us. She could hang with anyone while I was more to myself. I guess you could say I was socially awkward. A lot of people mistook it for me being scary, but it wasn't even that. I didn't like drama or bullshit and being around people brought both.

I didn't start going to parties or really speaking to people until Drea came to live with us. As you could imagine, I only went because she wanted me to. The truth of it all was I worried about Drea.

Although she lost her mama, she acted like it didn't bother her.

Whenever we brought auntie up, reminiscing or anything, she'd shrug it off. I knew it bothered her. If it didn't, she wouldn't act the way she does.

Why else would she party and drink so much? Why use men the way she does? Why is she so afraid to open up and talk about her mama? I mean, we were all grieving auntie's death. Yet we talk about her with no problem.

Splash!

"Agh! WHAT THE FUCK?" I screamed as I was soaked in chlorine filled water. I'd just bought this dress and now it was ruined. "Huuu!"

"Damn, my bad, lil' mama. I didn't notice you standing there." I heard the deepest, sexiest drawl I'd heard since...well...ever. "Let me get that for you. I can go dry it, come here."

Before I knew what was going on, he was standing in front of me and tugging on my dress, trying to get it off. I went into immediate panic mode. "Agghh! Get off me! Stop! What are you doing?" I was swinging hard as a windmill until I fell backwards into the pool. "Agghh! Help! Help! I'm drowning—help!" I was splashing and fighting to stay above the water.

Nobody knew this, not even Drea, but I didn't know how to swim. When we were little, we never had a pool or went to one. My mama was always afraid to let us go anywhere besides school and church. She feared we'd be snatched and killed like the kids our age on the news. When we did get wet, it was through some sprinklers in the neighborhood. Oh, and this one time. one of the boys in the hood broke the fire hydrant. We had a field day getting wet until the fire department came.

"Aye, mama, calm down, aight?" the same deep and sexy drawl was talking to me in a calm tone. Maybe if I knew him I would've felt comfortable enough to relax. Instead, I was freaking the hell out.

"Help me! Somebody, please!" My arms continuously flapped against the water as he did his best to get my wild anxiety under control.

"Aye, ma...hold on." Seconds later he jumped in the pool and grabbed me. "AYE! I need you to calm down, aight?"

I was taken aback by him yelling at me. I did settle down long enough to focus on his deep soft brown orbs. The longer I stared, the less frightened I became in his embrace.

"You aight, ma, okay?" His face was so close to mine I could smell the weed on his breath. Surprisingly, it helped soothe me. Normally, the smell of weed made me sick. "Look, you only in three feet, mama."

"I-I can't swim,"

"Aight, let me get you out of here then."

Why was I low-key mad he put me down when we got out the pool? Being in his arms had me in a comfortable trance. It was like having a bomb ass nap interrupted by the loud, obnoxious voice of an uninvited guest.

"Before you freaked out, I was trying to tell you I could dry your dress for you. Follow me in the house." He summoned, walking ahead of me. when he noticed I wasn't following him, he stopped and turned around. "You want to stay wet or not?"

"Nigga, I don't know you to be following you into that house. I'm good!" I think my bad energy was coming from him putting me down. Still, the fact remained that I didn't know him from an unmarked bullet.

"Shawty—"

"Excuse me, you don't know me, sir. I'm not a shawty or none of that shit you call these other bitches out here."

"Well how about sexy? Cause you sexy as hell." He flashed me a promising smile. Just like his eyes did before, his smile put me at ease. Moving from one leg to another, I felt my clit begin to throb. *Jesus, this man is fine!*

Taking in his full profile, I noticed he had medium warm brown skin and a thick but muscular build. Over in the shade by the pool his eyes looked dark brown. Now that we were in the light, I realized they were sandy brown, still calming. The way he held his red, thick bottom lip between his straight teeth, I wished it was my lip there. Even though he was rocking two gold teeth on the bottom row, it looked good on him. I was lost, mesmerized by his perfect eyes, smile, and physique. As good as he appeared, I just knew trouble came with him. If it wasn't the two tear drops under his left eye, it was the other tattoos littering his upper body that screamed 'Bitch, run the opposite direction. He don't mean you no good!'

Snapping out of my trance at that thought, I shook my head. I noticed the sun was about to go down and it was getting chilly out here. "Nawl, I'm good. Me and my cousin about to leave anyways. Bye!"

As I turned to walk off, I heard squealing and giggling. "Oh, my gawd! Boy, you play entirely too much!"

It was Drea. The guy that she met the other day when we were out to lunch had her in his arms. He was holding her over the pool's deepest level. She was squirming and giggling but that didn't stop me from rushing over there.

"Drea!" I didn't know why he had her like that nor did I care.

"Say you'll let me take out or else I'm dropping you," the guy taunted. By the sound of his voice, he meant business. Drea was just laughing and carrying o like he wouldn't drop her in the pool.

"Boy, please, I wish you w—aghhh! K, stop playing!"

"I ain't playing. That's one thing I don't do, ma."

"Huuu! Why you sweating me so bad? I told you I have a man." Drea was lying her behind off. She had a few dips, but none she was serious about. She just didn't want to get into nothing serious. That way she didn't have to rely on one source of income.

"I don't care about none of that shit. I told you I'm your man now." Okay, this dude was serious. I'd been standing there long enough. It was time for me to speak up.

"Excuse me, but can you put my cousin down? Drea, it's time to go!" I demanded with my hands on my hips, through my wet dress. The breeze from the wind paired with the wetness of the material clinging to my skin was making me cold and I began to shiver.

"What, Niya? For real? We just got here and I'm having fun!" she whined like a damn five-year-old. I hated when she acted like this when I was ready to go, and she was trying to stay somewhere.

"Yeah, Niya, she having fun with my brother. Plus, I still need to get your dress in the dryer." The guy who caused me to fall into the pool and also saved me said, walking up behind me. He was close enough to me that I felt his body heat, making me turn from cold to hot all over.

I spun around to face him and he grabbed me. "Whoa—"

"Don't touch me—aghh!"

Splash!

I fell in the pool again. "Help me!" My arms were flailing around in the water again, trying my best to stay afloat. Only this time, I truly thought I was about to die. Maybe it was all in my head, but I swore I felt my lungs flooding with water.

"Damn, Niya, you aight?" Drea asked with true concern. *This bitch. Here I am about to die and she's asking if I'm alright?*

"Fuck you, Drea!"

Splash!

"See? Looks like you're staying awhile. Might as well come inside and take off your dress," my lifeguard from earlier whispered in my ear after he scooped me up to carry me out the pool once again.

I couldn't even argue with him. I was going to be here until Drea was ready to go, whenever that was going to be. If I wasn't shit, I'd leave her ass here and let 'K' bring her home. I didn't know that nigga or his fine ass brother, so I wasn't leaving my cousin here by herself.

THREE

Kalib

"Hmp!" Lil' mama snatched her dress out my hands and tried to stomp off. Hence, *tried* to stomp off. I ran behind her and swooped my arm around her waist.

"Aye, Sexy, wait up. I just did you a favor." I reminded her. She spun around with fire in her eyes.

"Okay, and? The hell you want now? Some pussy?" She raised her eyebrows in a scowl. I smirked at her sexy ass. As tempting as that sounded, I wasn't that type of guy. I loved pussy like the next nigga, but I wasn't just busting any female down. I had a type and she was it.

She didn't know it, but I'd been watching her since she walked into the party. The way she walked demanded attention. Well that, plus she kind of had her nose stuck in the air. It was like she was silently screaming, "I don't belong here!" Though she was petite, she packed a lot of curves. I knew from the minute I laid eyes on her, her body would feel good against mines. I confirmed it when I retrieved her out of the pool—twice—and I didn't want to let her go either time.

Sexy had an attitude too. She knew she didn't want to get out of my strong arms. I'm not a cocky nigga, but I knew the facts. I mean, what woman wouldn't want to lay against a strong man? Then to know he wasn't hers was something else. I could be hers, but we had to work on her attitude first.

"What type of nigga do you think I am?"

"A nigga," she scoffed. "All y'all the same. Ain't good for shit."

"Well damn, Sexy. I thought I was good for a little something. I mean, I just helped you with your wet dress and all."

"Okay and I repeat, and? You keep bringing that up like I'm supposed to be thankful. You did *push me* in the pool, after all."

"Oh, so it's my fault you freaked out? I recall me accidentally splashing you. Not once did I touch you hard enough to push you in." I shook my head, lightly laughing. "You didn't even say thank you after I saved you from drowning."

She side-eyed me then rolled her pretty brown eyes. Then she muttered, "Thank you."

I heard her but wanted to play. "Huh? I can't hear you, Sexy."

"If you can huh, you can hear, nigga." I loved her little sassy attitude. It was a turn on more than anything. Still, I was going to get her shit right. I would only deal with her backlash for so long.

"Can you get out now? I need to put on my dress."

"You can put your dress on in front of me." I took a seat on the chaise lounge in front of the bed. We were in my room where I had given her a pair of my boxers and a shirt. She looked good in them too.

Her curves filled out my clothes. It was like she was born to wear my underwear. Like if she was my girl, I could get used to seeing her walk around the house this way.

"Fine. I'll go in the bathroom." She rolled her eyes before switching away.

I noticed she left her iPhone unlocked next to me. I took the initiative and added my number in her phone. I also texted myself from her phone save her as a contact.

"Have you seen my phone? I think I left it— What are you doing? Give me my phone!" She snatched it out my hands. "How did you even get in it? I bet you hacked it or some other criminal shit!"

"Damn, Sexy, that's what you think of me?" I smirked, watching her go through her phone like I put a virus on it.

"What's this?" She placed a hand on her hip and shifted her weight, pushing her phone in my face.

"Looks like my number, Sexy." I chuckled. Man, I bet this girl found anything to trip about. I didn't know her like that but could tell just by this small encounter.

"Who said I wanted your number...Kalib?"

"Kal-Lib not Kay-Leb," I corrected.

"Well, Kalib! Don't just be adding numbers in my phone." She rolled her eyes.

I fell over, laughing hard, as she stood in front of me with a hard glare. "You sexy. You do realize that, right?"

"Yeah. I don't need you telling me how I look though." She moved from one leg to another. I could tell I had her feeling some type of way.

"Why you so mean, huh? Who did it? I'll fuck them up because a woman as sexy as you should be happy and smiling."

"I am happy. I just don't know you and don't appreciate you touching my stuff."

I stood up and got in her personal space. "Then what can I touch?"

She stood there, staring at me at a loss for words. Her small but thick, soft looking lips were ajar. I couldn't help myself as I crashed my lips into hers. My hands found their way to her slender waist, following the maze to her thick hips and big soft ass.

I could tell she was into the kiss by the way she moaned and pressed her body against me. It was like she was waiting for me to make this move. I didn't put shit past a female. They played these types of games. Her mean girl attitude could've really been a front and she might be a gold digger.

"Ahh..." she breathed deeply when I slipped my hand up her dress. I snatched her panties off to gain access to her moist lips. She was so wet, I had to get a taste.

I dropped to my knees and pushed her dress up. I was faced with her pretty, bald pussy. The lips were wet and ready for me to kiss them into ecstasy.

Before I could bury my head between her legs, she pushed my shoulders and stared into my eyes. I could see the fear mixed with lust in them.

Gently removing her arms and placing them at her sides, I raised one of her legs and set it on my shoulder. I was about to let my mouth do some much-needed regulating.

"Oohhh, my g-g-g...fuck!" The way she cussed was cute as shit. If my mouth wasn't already full, I'd be laughing at her.

FOUR

Kanan

Shorty agreed to let me take her on a date but sitting across from her had me feeling some type of way. This was the first time I'd ever felt nervous around a chick. Yeah, we had a decent time at the backyard party, but I wasn't nervous then because I was around my people. Now that we were alone I barely knew what to say to shorty. I was sitting looking like a damn fool.

"You real quiet. Let me find out you shy in front of little ole me."

"Naw, I'm good, shorty. Just trying to see what I'm about to grub on. I'm hungry as shit. I ain't eat all damn day."

"So tell me about yourself, Kanan. Who is Kanan, what does he do? Give me the tea." I laughed when she said that last part. It was shit I heard my mom say all the time when she was on the phone with her friends.

"Ain't much to know about me, shorty. I'm twenty-seven, my favorite color black, and I got a brother." She smiled and took a sip of her red wine.

"None of that counts. I already knew all of that. Tell me something I don't know." *Her ass nosy as fuck.*

"What you the police or something, ma? Why you asking all these questions?" I didn't like to give away too much information about myself when I'd just meet a chick. Bitches be setting niggas up. I had to be cautious of what information I shared.

"You the one invited me here, and you sitting here acting like you not interested. I can take my ass right the fuck back home." She stood up from her chair and grabbed her purse.

"Sit down," I said in a nice, low tone. She looked at me and rolled her eyes then turned to walk off.

"Sit yo' ass down!" I demanded in a more aggressive tone. Now everyone in the damn restaurant were looking at us. I didn't give a fuck though. I would act a damn fool anywhere and not give a fuck who watching. "What the fuck you still standing for? Sit yo' extra ass down." She rolled her eyes again and then sat her ass back down.

"You making a damn scene in these people nice ass restaurant," she said while drinking the rest of her liquor.

"You making me make a scene. Doing all that extra shit ain't gonna fly with me, ma. Now you tell me about yourself. Let's start this shit over."

"Nothing to tell." *Now she got a funky ass attitude. I'm gonna have to get that shit in check.*

"Where you live? You live with yo' moms?"

"I don't have a mom."

"How the hell you get here then if you don't have a mom? What, a stork dropped yo' ass from the sky?" She tried not to laugh, but I could see the smile creeping on her face.

"She died a while ago."

"Damn, sorry to hear that." I could tell talking about her mom was a sensitive subject for her. I decided not to ask her anything else about it because I didn't want shorty to break out crying in the restaurant.

"Anyway, this shit is boring. Let's go somewhere and have some real fun. You like playing pool?"

"I can do a lil' something. Come on, let's bounce. I know a place we can go. We can get some wings and drinks there. I ain't feel like eating this plain ass food anyway. I'm high as hell I need some fried food."

"Let me drive."

"What? Hell naw, girl, this car too fast for you." *She must be crazy as hell if she think she about to drive my Maserati. Females don't even know how to drive.* Hell, I barely knew how to drive. I crashed more cars than I could count.

My brother and I own a few car dealerships throughout Atlanta. Our dad left us a shit load of his drug money, but we decided to do the opposite of what he did. Our dad was a certified street king that he ran the A. Everybody feared him, and because we were his sons, they feared us too. After our dad was killed, everyone expected us to take over his empire, but our mom begged us to take the straight and narrow path. Since we were momma's boys, we did as she asked. Besides, neither of us wanted to end up in jail or dead like our pops.

Our pops left us enough money to last a lifetime. Being from the hood, we decided to share the wealth with the people we grew up with. We did a lot of charity work for the neighborhood shelters and we gave back to the kids. Man, we love the kids in our old neighborhood. They're bad as shit, but we make sure they have a safe place to play and have the supplies they need to succeed.

We handle most of the transportation to get the foreign cars to our dealerships. Well, my brother does. He doesn't let me move the cars anymore because I crashed at least three cars speeding and one while drinking and driving. Because we own the dealerships, we could drive any car whenever we wanted. When I'm feeling good, I like to race. My ass would get behind the wheel and think I was a NASCAR race driver and shit. After I totaled a Benz, my brother told me I couldn't drive any car I didn't purchase for myself. I ain't fight him on it because he was my big brother and I knew his ass could beat me. I always put up a good fight, but he's a lot bigger and stronger.

"I'm a good driver, Kanan."

"Girl, yo' ass don't even have a car. Explain to me how you a good driver if you ain't driving?"

"Shut up! You gonna buy me car?"

"You gonna give me some pussy?"

"Really?"

"Yeah, really. How you expect me to get you a car and I ain't even smash yet?"

"And you ain't gonna smash either." I laughed hard as fuck when she said that. *She got me fucked up if she think I ain't hitting that.* It might not be today or even tomorrow, but I knew she was going to let me in that thang.

"And why you wearing this bright green ass, see-through cat woman suit? When you with me, you need to be classy. I don't need niggas staring at you while you with me. With them lil' ass titties."

"Ugh, shut up, K! My titties aren't that little. You being a bug right now."

"For real though, shawty. You a reflection of me now so don't wear that shit no more. I'm gone burn that shit when you take it off." Shawty had me fucked up if she thought she was going to be rolling around town with me with that shit on. She was trying to have me run a nigga over for looking at her ass and titties and shit. She was too sexy to be out here looking like a chicken head hoe.

We pulled up to the pool hall in Decatur where I grew up. It was a little ghetto and rough, but that's what I loved about it. It helped me remember where I came from. When I came here I always felt safe because my homies I grew up with own the spot.

"K, you ain't tell me you was rolling through. If you had told me, I would have had yo' favorite spot ready." I gave my homie Dean, the owner, a brotherly hug. Kalib and I gave him the money to buy this place. When the original owner died, they were going to close it down. Dean came to us and asked if we could front him the money to buy the place. Us being generous and loyal to where we came from, we never declined.

"It's a last-minute thing. My shawty said she wanted to play some pool and have a good time. You know this the only place I would recommend."

"Respect," Dean said while leading us to an available pool table. I grabbed our sticks while Andrea sat on the edge of the pool table with her legs wide open. I saw all the niggas looking at her with lust filled eyes. I didn't know if she trying to make me jealous or piss me off. Either way, that shit wasn't going to fly with me.

"Get yo' stupid ass down, girl." I snatched her by her arm and pulled her down from the pool table. I ain't mean to yank her so hard, but I'm a strong guy so some shit happened naturally.

"Boy, don't fucking grab me like that. You out yo' damn mind." I was glad the music was loud because if it wasn't everyone would have heard her yelling.

"Why the fuck is you sitting up there with yo' legs wide open? You want the whole damn bar to see yo' pussy?"

"If I wanted to, that's my damn business. Don't fucking put yo' hands on me like that."

"I barely touched you. Do some hoe shit like that again and you gonna feel more than a lil' grab on the arm." I didn't put my hands on women, but she needed a slap or two because she was acting up.

"I'm ready to go," she said with her arms folded and her lips poked out. She looked sexy as hell when she was mad. I couldn't help but smile at her fine ass.

"I don't know what you smiling for. Shit ain't funny."

"Come on, let me whoop yo' ass in pool first. Then I'll take yo' cry baby ass home."

"Fine!"

FIVE

Andrea

Kanan was a damn pain in the fucking ass. I tried having a good time on the date, but his ass was just plain rude. I wasn't going to drop him yet because it was too soon and I needed to run his pockets up. After I beat his ass in pool—twice—he got mad and dropped me home. I could tell he was a sore loser so I teased him the whole ride home. Instead of replying to my taunts, he kept saying I was his girl now and I'd better drop whoever I was dealing with. The shit tickled me because wasn't no way in hell I was dropping my hoes for him.

Sitting at my vanity, I was thinking about what my plans were for the day. I was off work and I didn't want to sit in the house all damn day. I knew Niya wouldn't go out with me since she came to the back-yard barbecue with me the other day.

"Hey cousin!" Aniya came in my room and flopped down on my bed. This was something she did all day, every day. She'd be so damn bored when we weren't at work. She lives vicariously through my life and would be blood thirsty to hear my stories. She never hesitated to give me her criticism. She just worried about me sometimes. I didn't know why because I knew how to take care of myself.

"What's up, cuz? Why you all smiles today?" Aniya had this smile on her face that I hadn't seen in a long time.

"Damn, I can't smile?"

"Sure, but you never do. Does this smile has anything to do with Kalib?"

"No!" She said it too fast, so I knew she was lying.

"Girl, that's a lie and the truth ain't in you."

"Well, he has been blowing me up. I haven't really replied to any calls or text. He's very persistent."

"Girl, so is his damn brother. He keeps saying I'm his girl. If he starts fronting me that cash, I will definitely be his girl. He rude as fuck though. He doesn't care what the hell he says out of his mouth. I'm used to being the outspoken one, but his ass takes the cake."

"When you going out with him again?"

"I don't know. I'm playing the hard to get game right now. The more I play hard to get, the more he will want me. I guess you can say I'm acting like you." I said pointing to her.

"I don't be acting though. I really don't be wanting these clown ass dudes."

"So what you doing tonight? Maybe we should see if they want to double date or something." I don't even know why I suggested that. I knew her ass was going to say no.

"I'm chilling with my mama tonight. Maybe you could come with us. We going to see that new movie with Gabrielle Union."

"Naw, I don't want to mess up y'all mother and daughter time. I'm gonna find one of my lil' shawtys to take me out to dinner." I hated intruding on my cousin and aunt's mother daughter time. Even though they let me know all the time we are family and I wasn't intruding, it never felt that way. They always laughed and talked about shows and gossip that I didn't even know about. The shit made me feel like a third wheel. I'd rather stay home than feel like that.

"Drea, I really wish you would stop doing that. We grew up

together. We're practically sisters. You're never a burden or third wheel."

"I just want to chill. I really don't feel like sitting in a movie theater for three hours. I'm starving like Marvin."

"Well if you change your mind, we're going to be leaving in a couple of hours."

"Ok, cousin." She got off my bed then walked out the door. I was happy she left my room. I didn't feel like talking anymore.

I didn't have my mom in my life like Aniya had hers. I wasn't trying to be rude, I just didn't like going out with them. We chilled at home a lot, and that was enough bonding for me. I figured they felt sorry for me sometimes, but I didn't need anyone's sympathy.

My thoughts were interrupted when my phone began to ring. I looked at my phone and it was Kanan calling me.

"Hello."

"What you doing, shawty?"

"Shit."

"Where you at?"

"Home. Why?"

"I'm about to come grab you."

"Why? I don't feel like going anywhere," I lied.

"Be ready in thirsty minutes." I couldn't even respond because his ass hung up the phone on me. I wondered where the hell he was taking me. I knew one thing, food better be involved. I looked through my closet to see what I had ladylike to wear.

The other night we went out he told me to dress classy. I was going to do whatever he said for me to get in them pockets. I decided to go with a pink, long sleeve, off the shoulder, knee length dress. This was as classy as I was going to get for him.

As soon as I was done getting dressed, he texted me, letting me know he was outside. I didn't know why but a sense of nervousness suddenly hit me. I hoped he liked my dress. If he didn't, he could kiss my ass.

"You looking cute. Where you going?" My aunt asked when I

stepped out of my room. Aniya was sitting on the couch staring me down.

"Out with a friend. Y'all enjoy y'all movie date." I waved goodbye and walked out the door. When I stepped out, Kanan was leaning against a beautiful old school all black Chevy. *Damn. Where the hell this nigga get these cars from?* He was looking good as hell in his all black. He had on a black button-down shirt, black jeans, and all back loafers. I didn't know what brand the shoes were but they looked expensive.

"Damn, girl, you looking fine as fuck. I like the hair." He hugged me tight, and I damn near came in my panties when he kissed my neck. He smelled so damn good.

"You look nice too. I like the old school. Can I drive it?"

"Get in, Andrea." I got chills when he said my name. I liked a man that could put me in my place.

"So where we going?" I was excited to know where he was about to take me.

"You'll see, baby. Just sit back and relax." I did what he told me while watching him drive. *Damn, this man is fine as fuck.* That's all I thought as he drove us to our destination. "Why you staring at me, girl?"

"I'm not staring."

"I see you burning a hole in my damn face, shawty." I smiled and looked straight ahead. My eyes widened when he pulled in an outside movie theater. I hadn't been to one of these since I was a child. My mom used to take me every Sunday because it was free for children. That was the most positive thing I remembered about my mom.

"Oh, my god! I haven't been to one of these in years. I ain't know they still have drive-in theaters." Kanan let the top down on his car and grabbed a blanket off the backseat. It was a little chilly tonight. If I knew this is what we were going to be doing, I would have put on a jogging suit.

"Yeah, this where I bring all my new bitches." I gave him the dirtiest look I could when he said that.

"I'm just fucking with you, shawty. I just found out about this spot. One of my buddies said him and his wife come here a lot. I was gonna come alone, but I thought of you."

"Aww, how sweet."

"Let's go get some food before the movie starts." He hopped out the car then came around to help me out. He was being such a gentleman. We walked toward the theater concession stand and all eyes were on us. I didn't know if I was looking real mommyish or he was just well known, but I was loving the attention. He grabbed my hand and pulled me closer to him. I guessed he wanted to let everyone know I was his.

When we got to the counter, I felt someone staring at me. I looked to my left and there stood Darius. Darius was one of the dudes I fucked with on a daily. He often paid my phone bill and took me shopping here and there. We never established a relationship. We were just kicking it, and we both knew where we stood with each other. He had some chicken head hoe with him. If she was cuter, I might've been jealous but her ass was busted. I knew he wasn't going to say shit to me because he was with ole girl.

"What you want to eat, ma?"

"I'll take some popcorn and a lemonade." He placed our order, as I strolled through my Facebook timeline.

"Add me on Facebook." He snatched my phone out of my hand and went to add himself.

"Yo' ass is so damn rude." I snatched my phone back and looked through his profile. *Ohhh, so this is how he keeps flipping cars... He owns a dealership? Damn, he definitely got money. I done hit the jackpot with this one!* "You own a dealership?"

"No, I own many dealerships," his smart mouth ass said with that sexy ass grin on his face.

"You can get me a car for free then."

"Whatever you want, baby girl."

"Yeah, sure, Kanan." He laughed then grabbed our food from the cashier that I noticed was eye balling him since we walked up. *Hoes be so disrespectful.* I could've been his wife, and this bitch didn't even care by the way she was sexing him with her eyes. When we got back to the car, the movie was just beginning. I dug into my popcorn and got comfortable. He put his arm around my shoulder and pulled me closer to him. He pulled a blunt from behind his ear that I never noticed was there.

"You smoke?" he asked while lighting the blunt up.

"Yeah, sometimes." I smoked weed when I felt like it. I wasn't an everyday smoker or one of those people that had to have a blunt for breakfast, lunch, and dinner. He passed the blunt to me and I took a few pulls then passed it back to him.

"Damn, you sexy as fuck." I blushed then turned my attention back to the movie. He turned my face back toward him and kissed my lips. His lips were so smooth and soft. After a few pecks, he put his tongue in my mouth and we started devouring each other. He got my pussy dripping wet, and at this point, we were about to go all the way. He grabbed me by the waist and sat me on his lap. He began kissing and sucking all over my neck. I unzipped his pants and his dick popped out. The shit was so big I wanted to hop off him and run the hell away. He had one of those long, thick porn star dicks and the shit had the nerve to be curved.

"I don't think I want to do this anymore," I said while staring at his huge penis.

"Come on, ain't no running now. I'm gonna take it slow, I promise." He said that like it was the hundredth time it fell from his lips. He ripped my thong off and slid on a condom. I was surprised they had condoms to fit his humongous ass dick. He lifted me up and eased me down onto his penis.

"Oh, my god! Noooo, I can't do this." The shit was painful as hell.

"Shhhhhh! I got you, baby. Just take a deep breath." He then slammed me down on his dick and I just about lost it.

"Ohhhhhh, shit, K! Yesssss, shit... Oh my, god!" He continued to lift me up and down on his dick. I just held on tightly while digging my nails into his neck and shoulders. The shit was painful, but the pleasure out weighted the pain.

"Damn, girl, you scratching the shit out me." He took my arms from around his neck and held them behind my back. I couldn't get away if I wanted to. As he held my arms with his right hand, he grabbed the back of my neck and pulled my face down for a kiss with his left hand. "Ahhhh, shit! This pussy good as fuck, girl. This shit dripping."

"K, please don't stop." Somehow, he managed to pull out and reverse our positions. He placed me in the seat on my knees and started hitting it from the back. His hands were on my shoulders and he was helping me throw this pussy back on him.

"Ahhhhhhh, shiiiittt!" I screamed as I came all over his dick.

"Ohhhhh, fuck I'm 'bout to nuttt." Kanan fell on top of me after he came, and we stayed that way until we caught our breath.

"Damn, shawty! You got the bomb on the pussy," Kanan said while lifting up and fixing his clothes.

"Can you take me home? I need to soak in a hot bath. That thing could kill someone. You need to go see about getting that shrunk." He started cracking up laughing, but I was dead ass serious.

"You can handle it."

"Yeah, whatever. Just take me home. My insides hurt." He continued to laugh as he pulled out the parking lot. The sex was awesome, but I didn't know if I was going to be able to take that shit again. I had to mentally and physically prepare myself for that dick.

SIX

Aniya

Kalib: *Hey sexy. Wyd?*
As I stared at his text, I didn't know if I wanted to reply. For the last few days, I'd been ducking and dodging Kalib's every call and text. I was too nervous to talk to him. I was embarrassed about what I let him do to me. Lord knows it had been so long since a man made me feel like he did that day of the backyard party. I felt like a hoe, letting him put his mouth on my body the way he did, even though he succeeded in relieving the pent-up tension I had from work.

"Niya, did you hear what I said?" my mama pulled me from my thoughts.

"What you say, mama?" I put my phone away and gave her my undivided attention.

"I said I want some more chocolate covered raisins. These are about to be gone by the time the movie gets started."

She was right because we both loved to mix chocolate covered raisins in our popcorn. "Okay, I'll go get some more."

We had a few minutes until the movie started anyway. We liked to get there early so we could pick our seats first. Mama liked to sit right in the middle. She said they were the best seats and she could see better that way. I had to agree and so did other patrons because they seemed to fill up quicker than the others.

After getting our raisins, I headed back to the movie room when I bumped right into a woman and who I assumed was her son. He couldn't be older than three or four. He was also a cutie with light brown skin and wild, soft curls spread around his head.

"I'm so sorry about that." The woman softly apologized. "KJ, apologize to the nice woman."

"Sorry," he softly spoke and then hid his face in the crook of the woman's knee. I giggled at his cute self. He had those kinds of cheeks you could squeeze and never get tired of kissing.

Seeing him made me think of my ex-fiancé, Arnell. People asked me why I turned my nose up at hoodlums and niggas that looked to be hood. Well, I lost Arnell to the streets. To be honest, I hated him for getting killed. I hated him for leaving me with such a huge whole full of judgement. It wasn't fair that I couldn't date a man without thinking the worst of him. Drea loved to call me stuck-up but it wasn't even that. I was just guarded.

"Aye, y'all wait up for me!" I heard a deep yet familiar voice echo from behind us. I turned and watched as the little boy, KJ, ran to none other than Kalib. I didn't know how to feel as I watched him interact with the little boy and his mother. I began to feel stupid and angry all in one. A part of me wanted to run up on him for an explanation while the other said to run away.

I guess I stood there too long. He looked up from his family and noticed me watching them. "Niya? Aye, wassup, sexy?"

I hated that his smile made me want to smile. It made me want to melt. It made me want to float over to him. Instead of doing any of that, I ran in the opposite direction. I ran far and fast to the other side of the theatre and didn't stop until I felt like I was safely hidden from his eye. I found a private bathroom and locked myself inside.

"Okay, Niya. Breathe, girl. He ain't your nigga. You can't be mad. He obviously has a wife and son. You had no business letting him between your legs without knowing his ass. It's your fault, girl." I was pacing around the stall, talking to myself. I had so many emotions sprinting through me. The biggest one was regret.

After gathering myself, I peeked out the door to make sure the coast was clear. Once I was satisfied, I went back to my movie. I was surprised it still hadn't started but happy at the same time.

"What took you so long?" my mama asked when I sat down.

"Girl, it was a long line." I played it off, shaking my head.

"I bet it was, girl." She chuckled. I loved my mama and the time we spent. I wished Drea would've came with us. It was like anytime me and mama went out to do something she never wanted to join us. I hated that me and mama had to beg her, but it was what it was.

While the previews were playing, I took the time to turn off my phone. Not before I noticed three missed calls and two texts from Kalib though.

Kalib: *Sexy, why you run away like that?*

Kalib: *Who you here with? What movie theatre you in?*

I scoffed as I went ahead and cut off my phone. *Why does he want to know who I'm here with and what movie I'm seeing? He got a whole family. Boy bye, you can miss me with that.*

A WEEK LATER...

I was in a deep, comfortable sleep when I heard loud knocking on my door followed by Drea's screaming.

"Niya! Wake up, bitchhh!" She barged in, jumping on my bed like a maniac.

"Huuu! Drea, go away! This my day off. I just want to sleep." I'd had a long week at the call center and was drained. If I wasn't training someone, I was firing them. Ben had me doing his job while he sat on his ass. I was so over my job. I might've gotten paid good, but I wasn't happy with my job. Every day it was some new mess.

"Girl, you can sleep when you dead! We got to get to McClain's Dealership!" Drea was hyped.

I pulled the covers back, glaring at her with a side-eye. "Why?"

"Girlll, K giving me a car! Now come on and get up before he changes his mind!" She ran out the room before I could protest. I had so many questions and things to say. *K giving her a car?*

Drea had been seeing Kanan almost every day since the backyard party. I never stuck around long enough to watch them interact, but Drea always had a story. If they weren't going on a date somewhere, they were laid up at his crib. Now he was giving her a car? I wasn't mad at all. I was used to this with Drea by now.

I think she liked him more than she did any trick she'd been with. When she talked about him, she smiled all hard. Sometimes I'd hear her on the phone with him and a few times he came and picked her up at work for lunch. That was different. She never let a dude come up to the job.

An hour later we were pulling up to the dealership. The whole ride there, Drea was hype as hell. Plus, we were blasting *Invasion of Privacy* the entire ride. The whole album was a vibe, so you couldn't help but be hype listening to it. When "I Like It" came on, both of us went stoopid. I couldn't help it. This song made me come out my shell.

"I said I like it like that!"

"Oh, he so handsome what's his name?"

"I said I like it like that!"

"Oh, I need the dollars!"

"I said I like it like that!"

As we were getting out, K met us outside, singing. "Cómo mueve el culo lakaka awashawawa! I say I like it like that! Yasss, girlllaa!" He struck a pose, causing Drea and me to fall out laughing.

"You so crazy!" Drea jumped into his arms and he spun her around, kissing her all over her face. Drea was squealing like a little kid on a playground. I sat back and watched them go at it with a huge smile on my face. Seeing them together was nothing compared to the stories. They had me believing they knew each other all their lives.

"Oh, hold on, baby!" Drea moved out his embrace and pulled him over to me. "I know you remember my cousin Niya. Niya, you remember K?"

"Yeah, I remember shawty." K was cracking up like something was that funny. "Aye, you learn to swim yet?"

See I was going to be nice to this nigga for Drea, but he could kiss my ass now. "Ugh, forget you!"

"Forgotten, shorty." He flashed me a slick grin before pulling Drea away to the car lot. I shook my head at his rude ass.

Ugh, Drea sure knows how to pick them. I was getting back into my car about to home.

"Sexy? Is that you?" I heard and smelled him before I saw him. I didn't stop to turn and get a look at him. I knew he was probably looking finer than ever so I acted like I didn't hear his ass.

Before I could fully shut my door, he grabbed it and swung it open. "Kalib, what are you—"

"Oh, so you do know who the fuck I am?" His voice carried an octave, but he didn't exactly yell. Instantly, I felt myself creaming in my panties as a shiver ran through my body.

Still, I wasn't about to let him see me sweat. "Boy, bye. I don't know who you think you talking to—"

"I'm talking to you, Aniya!" This time he kept his voice low but spoke with so much force. "What's up with you ducking and dodging my calls and texts, huh? It's been two fucking weeks and I ain't heard from you."

"Okay, and?" I snapped, rolling my eyes. "Why you worried about me? Don't you have a girl and a kid? You can miss me with all—"

"Fuck you talking about? I ain't got no damn girl or kid. What kind of nigga you take me for?" He looked to be offended.

"A nigga, that's what!"

"Who told your ass I had a kid and a girl?" He moved into my personal space. Smelling his cologne and feeling his breath against my skin was making me feel all types of ways. I was determined not to let him know what I was really feeling.

"I saw it with my own eyes at the movies last week! You were with your girl and kid, the little boy KJ. He looks just like you." Saying those words out loud helped me remain mad at him. I was mad because he led me on. He ate my pussy so good, making me want more. All along I couldn't have him.

He shook his head and softened his tone. "Naw, ma. You got it all wrong. That's my sister-in-law and nephew, that's my big brother's family. He on lock down right now, so Kanan and I try to spend as much time as we can with him. Usually, my sis don't tag along but she wanted to get out the house that night."

I sat there feeling like shit as he explained all that to me. I was seriously at a loss for words. Hanging my head, I couldn't bring myself to even look him in the eyes. This whole time I'd been avoiding him all because I thought he was married with a son. Lord, I knew he was thinking I was a nutcase now.

I wasn't expecting him to lift my chin and stare me in the eyes so boldly. He licked his lips and said, "Sexy, if I had a family, I wouldn't even waste your time like that. I damn sure wouldn't be blowing you up like a hoe. I ain't going to lie, I felt like a bitch after what went down at the party and you not answering my calls. I can honestly say I know how a woman feels when men do that shit to them. I ain't gon' never do that shit to another woman 'cause it's a fucked up feeling."

I couldn't help but crack a smile and laugh. He just said some deep stuff. It was true though. "What? I'm serious, Sexy."

"I'm sorry for assuming without asking you first, Kalib. I should've known better."

"Naw, you didn't know any better. It's like you said, I'm just a nigga to you. I wanna show you I'm a man though." He caressed the side of my face. "Can I show you I'm a man, Sexy?" Without hesitation, I nodded my head and replied, "Yes."

SEVEN

Andrea

Sitting in Kanan's room on his bed, I started to get a feeling. My nosey ass had never been in a man's house alone before. I decided to get up and go through his closet and drawers. *Damn, he definitely got a lot of clothes.*

"What the fuck you doing?" I jumped at the sound of Kanan's deep voice.

"I was just looking around," I said while speed walking out of the closet. He followed behind me and closed his closet doors behind him.

"What yo' nosey ass doing today?"

"I don't know. I guess I'm gonna go home. I've been here for damn near a week. I need to see what my cousin's up to. I haven't seen her in days, so I know she misses me. You made me use all my vacation days at work."

"Man, she ain't thinking about you. My brother got her occupied."

"I don't think so. Aniya doesn't date. I don't know how many times I tried to get that girl out the house."

"Well my brother got this type of affect that drives women crazy."

"I guess. Can you take me home now? I don't have any more clothes."

"Andrea! You forgot I just bought yo' ass a brand-new Audi?"

"Damn, I definitely forgot. I thought that shit was a dream. I haven't drove it anywhere but here. We've been locked up in this house since you got me the car." I felt dumb as hell. *How could I forget this man just bought me a brand-new Audi truck?* I couldn't believe he really got it for me. I was kidding when I kept telling him to get me a car.

"So when you coming back?" he asked while pulling me on his lap. He was kissing the back of my neck and my shoulders. I needed to get the fuck out of here before we were fucking again.

"I don't know, Kanan. I have to go back to work on Monday."

"Well today is Friday. Get some clothes and come back. You can go to work from here."

"Ok." I gave him a kiss on the lips and hopped off his lap. It was time for me to drive my damn car. *I can't wait to make all those hating ass hoes on my block jealous.* I used to always get into it with bitches on my block because their men always tried to talk to me. *It ain't my fault I'm fine as fuck.* When they saw me pull up in this new all black Audi truck, I knew they were going to start spreading rumors.

I RODE through my block for the hundredth time, blasting my music. Like usual, it was niggas on every corner. I smiled at a few bitches that I knew didn't like me because of their man. Of course, they rolled their eyes and gave me dirty looks. I was loving every minute of it. I finally got tired of driving so I parked my car in the back of our apartment building. Ain't no way in hell I was parking my shit in the front. Bitches wouldn't hesitate to key my brand-new car.

When I walked through the back door of our apartment that was attached to the kitchen, I wasn't surprised to see my aunt in there cooking. Some working women cook only three times a week. Nope, not my aunt. She made sure it was a hot meal on the stove every single day.

"Hey, baby. Where you been all week?" My aunt asked while giving me a hug.

"At a friend's house."

"Ummmmmm hum. Well I missed seeing your face. Don't be leaving this house that long without calling me. You know I worry about you girls."

"Auntie, you could have called me."

"Did a few times and it went straight to voicemail."

"Aww, sorry. My phone was probably dead."

"Niya's in there watching *Black Ink Crew Chicago*. Gone in there, dinner is almost done." I walked into the living room and Aniya was sitting on the couch shaking her head.

"What's up, cousin? What you shaking yo' head for?" I took a seat next to her on the couch and watched the tv with her.

"Girl, do you know Ryan's ass done fucked up the whole shop? Then had the nerve to get a whole new shop and new tattoo artists." She said referring to one of cast members.

"No, the fuck he didn't, bitch." I kicked my shoes off and gave the television all my attention. These were times I cherished the most with my cousin. This was the only thing Niya really liked to do so I tried to engage as much as possible.

"So how you liking yo' new ride?"

"Girl, I love it! I still can't believe that man got me a whole damn car. A nigga ain't never gave me more than five hundred dollars."

"I think he really likes you. Kalib told me he talks about you all the time."

"Kalibbbbbb? Ohhhhhhh, I see you, girl! You liking all up on Mr. Kalib McClain, ain't you?"

"Girl, shut up. I hate you." Niya couldn't help but smile anytime she talked about Kalib. I was happy my cousin was out here getting some action. I knew she stressed out about work and shit so she needed a man in her life.

"You want to go to the club with me tonight?" I asked Aniya, hoping she would be up for it.

"Girl, now you know I am not going to a club. Besides, Kalib is supposed to be coming over later to watch movies and chill."

"Damn, you got that man coming to the hood for that hot box." We both fell back laughing on the couch. We always had good laughs together.

"My mama wants meet him. She said it's too much bad shit going on in the world for her not to know who I'm dating." My auntie was always paranoid about something.

"First of all, if she stops watching that damn ID channel and *Snapped* she wouldn't be so damn scary and paranoid."

"I hear you in there talking that mess, little girl. I watch what I want!" My aunt yelled from the kitchen.

"Well, I guess I'll get Whitney and Charmaine to go out with me tonight. I have my own car now and I'm not about to sit in the house and waste a good weekend." Whitney and Charmaine were two chicks we went to high school with. They were cool or whatever. We weren't besties, but we did hang out a lot. They'd been somewhat loyal so whenever I called them to go out they'd be down for it.

"Gone head, girl, because I ain't going," Aniya said while texting in her phone. I knew she was texting Kalib because she was smiling from ear to ear. I went to my room to find what I planned on wearing to the club tonight. As I looked through my closet, a text notification came to my phone.

K: Aye. Where the fuck you at girl?
Me: Home.
K: Hurry up and bring yo ass back.

I ignored Kanan's last text and continued to find something to wear. I wasn't going back over there right now. As much as I loved laying around in his nice, big ass house, I refused to let this Friday night go to waste. I texted my home girls and let them know I was picking them up in my new Audi truck. They both were thirsty as hell to see my car. More so because they thought I was lying.

After tearing my closet apart, I finally found the perfect outfit. I chose this cute little black beaded skirt with a black see-through crop top. *This shit gonna compliment my car well.* I took a shower, got dressed, and headed to pick up my ladies.

"BIITTTCCCHHHHH, this car fly as fuck! How many dicks you sucked to get this?" Charmaine said while racing Whitney for the front see. Charmaine and Whitney are those type of friends that's really not your friend. They sneak diss and talk shit about me, but I don't care. I just need extra bitches with me in case a fught break out.

"Bitch, my new boo gave me this car." Speaking of K, I looked down at my phone and he was calling again. This nigga was actually calling me back to back. *Is this motherfucker crazy or something? I will call him back after I leave the club.*

When we pulled up to Magic City, it was a long ass line as usual. I pulled up to the front so valet could park my car. When we hopped out, all eyes were on me. Not us. Me, baby. I was soaking in all the attention. A bitch felt like a celebrity.

"Damn! Y'all can come through V.I.P. Right over here, sexy." The bouncer called out to us. We happily walked over and into the club. We were excited because we never got a chance to come through V.I.P.

"Damn, this bitch lit tonight!" Charmaine screamed over the music. The club was packed and it was damn near dark. If it wasn't for the stage lights we all would be walking in the damn dark. The shit was kind of freaking me out, but all I need is liquor and I will be good to go. We went to the bar and started taking Henny shots. We were having a good time dancing and getting fucked up.

"Look, those dudes waving for us to come to their section," Whitney said while fixing her hair.

"Come on, let's go," I said while grabbing my drink from the bar. When we reached their section, I noticed all they asses were butt ass ugly. I wanted to turn around and run, but that would have been rude.

"Y'all ladies looking good. Come sit down with us for a minute." The ugliest dude out the pact said. We all took a seat and I made sure to sit on the far end of the couch so they couldn't touch me. Whitney was all in one of the dude's face. He wasn't that ugly but he wasn't fine. I decided to take my phone out and take some pictures for my social media.

"Let's go live, bitch," Charmaine said while snatching my phone out my hand. I hadn't gone live in a minute so I was down. I was looking good as fuck, and people needed to see this.

EIGHT

Kanan

M*an, this girl got me so fucked up.* I'd been calling her ass all damn night but she hadn't been answering. When I finally decide to stop calling, I got bored and got on Facebook. As soon as I logged in, all I saw was Drea on Facebook Live, shaking her ass in a see-through skirt. My blood pressure shot through the roof when I saw that video. I knew exactly what club she was at because my ass went there at least three times a week. I threw some clothes on then called my homie to take me to Magic City. I ain't want to drive my whip because I was about to snatch the fucking keys to the brand-new car I'd just bought Drea. I spent thousands on that car for shawty and she wanted to sit around and ignore my calls? Naw, shit didn't work that way with me.

We sat outside the club for two hours, smoking blunts as we waited for Andrea to come out. I needed to simmer down before my ass was in jail tonight for a domestic dispute. I watched closely as people started leaving the club. When my eyes landed on Andrea, I was pissed. Her outfit looked more revealing than on Facebook. I hopped out the car and went to lean on the front of the hood. I knew she was going to see me because she had to walk past my way to get her car. She was just laughing and smiling with no care in the world. I put my hands in my pockets to avoid knocking her ass to the ground.

"Girl, tonight was fun as hell. I missed you bitches," Andrea said to the chicks that was with her.

"Girl, yo' boo been calling all night. Is that where you about to go?" one of the girls asked.

"Girl, fuck him. I'm tired, I'm not driving all the way to his crib tonight. I'll see him tomorrow. He will be fine."

"Ah, yeah? Fuck me, huh?" She jumped when she heard my voice. She turned around and looked at me dumbfounded. She had this terrified and embarrassed look on her face.

"You following me now, K?" I couldn't believe this bitch was trying to flip the script right now.

"Don't fucking play with me, Andrea. I been calling and texting yo' dumb, stupid ass all fucking night! You too busy shaking yo' ass for Facebook. And what the fuck is you wearing?"

"Kanan, I was gonna come back with you. I just wanted to spend some time with my friends."

"Then that's all you had to say. Instead, yo' ass lied. Then you don't pick up yo' fucking phone." Now I was yelling and walking all in her face. I could tell her friends were getting scared, but I didn't give a fuck about them hoes.

"You need to calm yo' ass down. You doing way too fucking much right now." I had to rub my temples before I knocked her fucking head off.

"Go get the whip, shawty," I said while still rubbing my temples. All three of their asses hurried off. When they came back, I was confused as to why her friends were in the car.

"I'll meet you at your house after I drop them off," Andrea tossed out the window. I swung the driver's door open so fast I almost snatched that motherfucker off.

"Get the fuck out!" I yelled to all their asses.

"Are you serious right now, Kanan?" Andrea asked with that dumbfounded ass look on her face again. I reached over and snatched the keys out the ignition, and she saw that I was serious then. They all got out but I drug Andrea to the passenger's side and threw her in the car.

"How are we supposed to get home?" one of her hoe ass friends asked.

"Bitch, walk, get an Uber. I don't give a fuck how you get home." I hopped in the truck and pulled off. I looked in my rearview mirror and saw my homie helping those hoes get in his car. He was a good dude because my ass wasn't taking them nowhere.

"I really can't believe you right now, Kanan."

"Andrea, just shut the fuck up before you make me do something to yo' ass." I needed this ride home to be silent while I gathered my thoughts. *She must think I'm some type of lame or something.* I liked Andrea a lot but I wasn't about to let no bitch play me.

When I finally pulled up in front of Andrea's crib, her ass was knocked out. I sat there and looked at her for a moment. She was beautiful as fuck, but the shit she wore and the way she acted wasn't some shit I could get with. When we were chilling by ourselves, we had a good ass time. I loved seeing her in her pajamas, just lying next to me smoking weed and watching funny movies. Her ass got high off two pulls. The shit was so funny because she acted real silly when she smoked weed. It was those chill in the house moments I fucked with the hardest. I didn't mind her going out with her friends. I just didn't want my girl in revealing clothes and rejecting my calls. Was that too much to ask?

"Andrea." She opened her eyes and smiled at me. I wished I could be nice right now but fuck all that. I was still pissed, so she could slide the fuck out of this car.

"I'm sorry, baby."

I don't give a fuck.

"You home." She looked out the window then turned back to me with her face balled up.

"I thought we were going to yo' house?"

"Naw, I'm a holla at you though." That was my way of saying get the fuck out. She ain't say shit else.

She hopped out the car and slammed the door. *Fuck she so mad for?* I'm the one that was supposed to be mad. I needed time to think about what the fuck I was going to do.

I'd just bought this girl a whole damn car, and she was already acting a fool. Who did shit like that? If a motherfucker I damn near just met bought me a car, I would be worshipping the ground they walked on. But not Drea.

NINE

Aniya

The last man I had meet my mama was the man I thought I would be marrying so you could imagine how nervous I was right now. It was a Friday night and Kalib would be arriving soon.

As I looked over my outfit one more time, my nerves began to get the best of me. I had selected a pair of cotton grey leggings and a white tank top that clung to my curves with a pair of my Fenty slides. We were just having dinner with my mama and then Kalib and I were going to Netflix and Chill in my room. As bad as I wanted to feel his lips on me again, I wasn't going to let it go that far tonight. I mean for one, my mama's room was right next door. Two, I didn't want him to get too attached and get the wrong idea. Kalib and I were just friends. Just 'cause he tasted the goodies didn't mean a thing. That was the first and last time.

"Niya! Your friend is here, baby, come down here!" I heard my mama yell from the bottom step after the doorbell rang. I giggled on my way out the room, thinking about how she would call Drea and I from the bottom of the stairs to come eat when we were little.

Walking past Drea's door, I peeked in her room but didn't see her inside. The last time we talked was yesterday. She was pissed with Kanan and said she was going to see one of her old hoes. As always, I shook my head and laughed it off. I didn't care what Drea said. That girl was feeling Kanan more than a little bit. She was just in her feelings because he knew how to handle her. Drea was used to checking the guys she dated, not them checking her. My baby cousin probably felt like a weak hoe out here right about now. *I think she met her match with Kanan.*

"Damn, Sexy, you look good. Those pants were made just for you," Kalib complimented after I opened the door and let him in. I was blushing hard with a big smile on my face. I swore this man loved to gas me. We'd been talking on the phone nonstop since we got everything cleared up with us. He would call me in the middle of the day and we'd be on the phone for hours, laughing and talking about anything that came up. Kalib was starting to feel like the best friend I never had but always wanted.

"Why you way over there? Come give your man some love." He pulled me into his embrace and then tried to lay a kiss on my lips. I turned my head so he could have my cheek. "It's like that?"

"When did we establish I was your woman and you were my man? And I'm not kissing you when my mama is right in the next room."

"Shit, mama can get a kiss too." I wanted to think he was joking but nothing about his expression displayed that he was.

"Boy, bye." I laughed, putting my hand in his face.

"Mhm, keep on," he warned, smacking me on the ass.

"Kalib, chill on doing that in front of my mama. Damn, haven't you ever met a woman's mother before?"

His expression softened some. "Honestly, Sexy? Naw. I ain't found a shawty I felt was worthy of getting my time like you. I don't mean to be disrespectful in your mom's house. It's just I missed your sexy ass and can't help but touch you when I see you."

I was flattered by his honesty. "I feel you. That's fine and all but keep your hands to yourself for the next hour and a half, okay?"

"Damn, you say that like you got plans and shit." His lazy grin had me dripping in my panties. I knew I'd be changing my bottoms by the end of the night.

"Boy, shut up and come in the kitchen." I led him into the kitchen where my mama was putting the finishing touches on the food. "Mama?"

"Yes, baby?" She never bothered to look up. She was focused on taking whatever she had cooking out of the oven. Whatever it was, it smelled good and I was ready to eat.

"This is Kalib. Kalib, this is my mama, Anita," I introduced. Kalib took my mother's hand into his and kissed the back of it.

"Oohhh! Aren't you just the perfect gentleman? Ooohh, and you fine! No wonder why my daughter can't stop smiling and talking about you! Mhm, I see indeed." I was looking at my mama all crazy in the face when I noticed she was flirting with Kalib like I wasn't in the kitchen with them. Kalib was just standing there, staring at me with a goofy smile. I could feel his brown orbs burning into the side of my face as I looked everywhere but at him. I felt like if I looked his way I would die of embarrassment. It'd been a long time since I had a man or gave a man my attention. This was fresh and exciting for me. You damn right I was dancing around the house and at work. I was always smiling and laughing. I forgot how good it felt to feel thus way about a man. Now that I thought of it, I needed to thank Drea for making me go to that backyard party.

"So you been talking about me to moms, huh?" Kalib leaned down to whisper in my ear. His lip against my skin sent shivers up and down my spine. I had to move away.

"Mama, Kalib is a car salesman. He and his brother own a car lot." I changed the subjected in order to get the heat off me. Kalib wasn't slick. He knew what he was doing.

"Aw, okay! So you're fine, a gentleman, and got a job. I need me one of you! You got any brothers?"

"Mama!"

"What? Mama got to have a life too, right?"

"Mama!" I narrowed my eyes at her. She put her hands on her hips and laughed. She was fixing her lips to say something, but Kalib cut in.

"Naw, it's okay, Sexy. Yes, mama, I have two brothers. They're both in relationships though."

"Are they married?"

"Mama!" I was getting upset because I couldn't believe the things coming out her mouth right now.

"Man, Sexy, chill out." Kalib came over and grabbed me around the waist. I ain't going to lie, it felt normal being in his embrace. Like I was meant to be there. I couldn't figure out why I felt this comfortable with a man and we hadn't known each other a whole month yet.

"One of my brothers is married and the other is seeing someone," he confirmed. I thought back to the woman I saw him with at the theatre. I was so sure that was his wife. I guessed looks could be deceiving.

"Well what about your daddy? He still with your mama?"

"Mama—" I felt Kalib's body tense up. "You okay?"

He was looking into space like he saw a ghost. I nudged to snap him out of it. "Huh? Oh, yeah, I'm good. Mama, my pops passed away some years ago."

My mother's hand went to her mouth. "I'm so sorry, baby."

"It's all good. I used to freeze up when someone would bring him up. I'm good now."

"How did you learn to cope with it?" I was asking because maybe he could help with getting Drea to cope with her mother passing.

"I went out and shot at the niggas that killed him." He stated with a tight jaw and hard stare. Me and mama clutched our imaginary pearls. His facial expression softened and he chuckled. "Chill, I'm just playing. I saw a therapist."

"Whew wee! Boy, you had me think like damn! He fine, a gentleman, got a job, and he a thug too? Sign me up to be your brother's next girl if this one ain't actin right."

"Mama!" I couldn't help but laugh. This woman was on a roll tonight, I swear. I hadn't seen her act like this in a long time, since my high school days. My mama was saved, sanctified, and holy ghost filled. She was acting all open right about now.

"What, girl? Quit saying 'mama' and not telling me what you want."

"You do know that Drea is the one that his brother is dating, right?"

"Aw, damn! Tell her I said, 'beat it blocker!'"

This time, instead of getting upset, I joined Kalib in laughter. My mama was a trip.

"AT&T call center, this is Aniya Boles. How may I help y—"

"Niya, man, fuck all that! Where yo' bop head ass cousin at?"

"Umm, who am I speaking to?" I didn't know if it was this phone or I truly didn't recognize his voice. Whoever it was had an attitude with Drea though.

"Man, you know who this is! I'm tired of y'all playing games, man. I bet she told you to play stupid. Tell her—"

I hung up the phone on his ass. This was a company phone so I knew the message was recorded. In training class, we were told to just hang up on customers like that.

Me: Come to my office girl.

Drea: Here I come.

Not even five minutes later, Drea was coming into my office. "What's up? What Ben bald ass say I did now?"

"Girl, come in here and close the door," I urged.

"Whats wrong, Niya? You pregnant again, huh?" She did what I said and came to sit in the chair in front of my desk.

I gave her the evil eye. She promised she'd never bring that up. We promised to take that shit to the grave.

"Bitch, no, but don't bring that up again. You know better."

"Sorry, cousin. I shouldn't have said that." She was sympathetic.

I was still irritated but there were more important matters at hand. "It's whatever. Who did you piss off so bad they calling here and going off? This nigga knows my name and everything. He came at me, calling you a bop and some more shit!"

She stared at the floor like she was trying to understand what I'd just said. "Girl, I ain't piss nobody off. Not that I know of."

"Could it be one of your dips? Who did you go out with last night?"

"Girl, I was out with Darius. He wasn't mad though."

I rolled my eyes and blew a breath of frustration. "Why are you still seeing that nigga? What happened with K? Y'all were doing well together."

"Girl, fuck Kanan, his mama, his grandma, and his brother! I was with Darius because I felt like it." She popped an attitude with me.

"Why you all mad at him? I thought he just bought you a car?" I pointed out.

"Yeah, well, I did too. That nigga took the car back. Now he wants to act like we all good with us. Like I said, fuck him. I'm done with his ass. It's probably him calling."

"What the hell, Drea?" I was getting a headache thinking about everything she just said.

"Anyway, are you done? These phones aren't going to answer themselves, you know?"

I nodded my head and placed my hands on my hips. "Yeah, go."

Once she was out of my office, I called Kalib. I had to get to the bottom of this shit with my cousin and his brother.

"What's up, Sexy?"

"You niggas think y'all slick! Y'all come into a woman's life, woo her with nice words and gifts, just to snatch shit away when it's not going your way? Like I said, just like a nigga! You—"

"Whoa, whoa, whoa! Sexy, chill the fuck out!" Kalib roared into the receiver. I was breathing hard from going off. I stood, pacing the floor.

"Niya?"

"What, Kalib!"

"Aye, calm that tone down. Whoever did it, take that shit out on them. I'm going to ask you what's wrong and you're going to *calmly* tell me what it is. The minute you start yelling, I'm hanging up. When I hang up, I'm coming to find your ass and it's a wrap, ma. You got me?"

I was dead quiet now. The way he just asserted things had me leaking and my voice was stuck in my throat.

"Aniya! Do. You. Hear. Me?"

"Y-y-yess."

"Aight then. What's going on, Sexy? Keep in mind that I'm a man of my word," he warned. I nodded like he could see me.

"Okay, so I'm at work and I get a call. The guy on the other end is going off, saying Drea is a bop and asking where she at. I'm confused as hell. This man called my personal phone at my desk. He didn't call me Aniya but Niya, so this shit is personal. I called Drea in here and asked her who she pissed off and she can't say. So I asked her about who she was with and stuff like that. She told me then I asked about Kanan. She said fuck him and everything he stands for pretty much.

Then she goes on to tell he's been blowing her up lately, but she's not taking his calls. She also told me that he took the car he got her back, which is some messed up stuff if you ask me! Anyway, I came to the conclusion that it's him that called my phone acting like a lunatic. If this is how you and your brother behave, you can miss me with that shit. I'm already over it, Kalib!"

The line was silent. I took the phone away from my ear to see if he was still there. I was hot when I saw the line was dead. I didn't even hear the phone hang up.

"Ughhh!" I tossed my phone on my desk. Snatching the office door open, I was struck by his scent first. Looking into his eyes, I could've melted. It was the hard expression he was giving me that made me snap out of it and pop an attitude.

"What are you doing here, Kalib? This is my job! You can't just—" He shut me up by colliding his lips into mine. He was pushing us further into the office. I had my eyes closed at first. That was until I heard the office door lock.

"Mmm—nooo! Kalib, stop it." I tried to push him off. The next thing I knew, he was picking me up and sitting me on the desk. I was kicking myself for wearing this damn pencil skirt, as he forced it up my legs and over my hips.

"Kalib, what are you—ahhh! Sss, my gawd!" He plunged his right index and middle fingers into my wet opening. I thought I was wet before. This wasn't wet. This was soaked!

Next he snatched my panties off and stuffed them into his pockets. Pulling my chair under him, he took a seat and scooted closer to the desk. The whole time he just stared into my eyes, not saying a word. I didn't know if it was pissing me off or turning me on more. The way he just busted in my office without notice, not saying a word, was so sexy but irritating. These McClain brothers were something else.

I wanted so badly to cuss and kick shit, but it was too late. He slid me to the edge of the desk and his face met my southern hemisphere.

Feeling his lips latch onto my clitoris, I was mesmerized and my thoughts went back to that day of the party. Kalib ate me so good I couldn't feel my legs for fifteen minutes. I needed assistance to stand and walk. When he was finished, I knew he knew because he left me on the bed to recuperate after cleaning up the mess he made between my legs.

"Kaliiiib!" I was brought back to my surroundings, feeling his tongue lightly flickering my clit.

"Keep calling my name like that, Sexy. I'm the only one you going to be calling like that. You feel me?" He went back to eating my pussy like it was his last super.

You damn right I felt his ass. How couldn't I?

TEN

Kalib

I had to get Aniya together. No lie, every time she popped an attitude with me I was coming and getting her right. So far, I'd tasted her twice. That one time at the party and just now in her office. I wanted to do it last night but her moms was sleep in the room next to her.

When Niya originally wanted me to meet her mama, I didn't want to. I almost told her no. She said I had to if I wanted to go any further with her. No woman had ever said that to me before.

Then I thought about how I'd been thinking so much about her and how much I wanted to see her again, so I was like 'fuck it'. I was happy that I met her mama now. Ms. Anita was cool people and her cooking reminded me of my mama's.

"You good now?" I'd just finished getting my sexy together. She sat up on the desk and gave me a satisfied smile and a nod.

"Yeah. I can't believe you came up to my job like this. Where were you the entire time I was talking to you on the phone?"

"I was on my way. I wanted to take you to lunch. I heard your attitude and knew I had to get you right before we went anywhere."

"You wanted to? So we not going to lunch now?" She had a sad look on her face.

"Naw, Sexy, we are. I just had to adjust your attitude first." I kissed her on the mouth. To my surprise, she grabbed my face as I was pulling away and slipped her tongue in my mouth.

"Well, damn. I must of did a good job, huh?" I joked when we finally broke for air.

"I like to taste myself after you've finished." She gave me a sexy smile. That statement alone had me ready to lay her pretty ass on this desk and put this dick in her life, but I didn't feel she was ready for that yet. Aniya already had an attitude problem. If I gave her this dick, she'd surely have one when she wasn't getting it.

"Alright now. You better chill out, Sexy. You ain't ready for this." I pressed my third leg against her exposed pussy.

"Naw, baby, I think it's the other way around."

"Oh, for real?"

"Mhm, you'll never be the same once I put this on you."

"See, I knew you was an angry freak."

Smack!

"Oww, damn, bae! I'm just saying you be mean as a snake sometimes. Why is that?" I looked deep into her eyes, but she looked away.

"I'm just guarded, that's all." She shrugged and looked back at me.

"Did somebody hurt you, Niya?"

The look in her eyes said it all but her response was the opposite. "No, I'm just like this. I don't mean to come off as a bitch at times. It just happens."

I wanted to probe deeper and ask her more. I noticed she looked bothered so I let it go. "Listen to me, Sexy. You don't ever have to feel guarded around me. You got me?"

"Do I? I thought you were married with a son." She smirked. Sexy had jokes and I was trying to be serious. Lightly, I chuckled.

"That's cute but you already know that story. I'm being for real."

"I hear you, Kalib." She nodded.

"No, I need you to feel me, Sexy."

"I already did feel you," she slyly replied and then kissed me before I could say what was on my mind.

Man, what am I going to do with this woman? I already saw she was hiding something. It was the way she loved to change the subject or joke when I was clearly being serious. I didn't take being taken for a joke lightly. As long as she was going to stick around, I was going to get her to understand that.

I WAS JUST FINISHING up my day at one of the dealerships, tired as hell. Running your own business was hard enough. Imagine the amount of work you have to put in when you had more than one. The plus side to it though, you could make your own hours. You didn't have to answer to anyone and it was rewarding when you did shit right.

Every day I thank God we didn't follow in my father's footsteps. Growing up, I watched my dad struggle the way he did with the drug game. Shit wasn't lovely at all. I mean, sure he got hella money, but that was about it though. The rest was just a grip of problems.

Once I was on the road, on my way home, Niya popped into my head. A smile curved my lips. Niya was truly a breath of fresh air for me. She already had me wanting to be a better man. Not only for myself but my brothers and future kids. Right when I was about to text her, a message came thru from my sis-in-law.

Nat: Hey. You busy?

Me: Naw. What's good?

Nat: I made dinner for KJ and me. He asked if you could come and eat with us.

I thought about what she was asking me. Of course, I wanted to see my nephew but I also wanted to see his future aunt. There was no guarantee Niya would even agree to come to my house. I damn sure wasn't trying to go to hers tonight. I was trying to do some thangs to her body. Some thangs that would have her screaming extra loud. The hood already knew my name. I didn't want them fucking with her because of me though.

Nat: It's fine if you don't wanna come over. Sorry to bother you.

Me: You ain't bothering me. I'm on my way now.

I hated when she said shit like that. I didn't know if it was to send me on a guilt trip or if she was popping an attitude. I'd told Nat how I felt about her feeling like she was a bother.

"Uncle! Uncle!" My nephew came running full speed to me when I let myself inside the house. He was waiting by the stairs. I bent down and held my arms out to hug him and he embraced me.

It always warmed my heart when I hugged him. Nat was pregnant with KJ around the time my big brother, Kaleef, went to jail. He got caught slipping with some heat in his car. Our last name being McClain, the cops already knew our pops. When Leef went to jail, they were convinced he had a gun for street purposes. Little did they know, Leef was the hothead of us all. He went off on the cops without a second thought. They not only added assault with a deadly weapon but armed robbery onto his shit. They had my brother fucked up. The best our lawyer could do was get his fifteen years knocked down to five. However, he reacted without much though. He got into a few fights and another year was tackled on to his sentence.

"How you doing, lil' man?" I kissed him on the forehead.

"Uhh, good!" He grinned. Whenever he grinned it meant he was up to no good.

"Mhm, let me find out. Where is mommy?"

"In the kitchen. I'm waiting for grandma to come get me."

"Grandma? I didn't know she was coming for you." This was news to me. Nat said her and KJ were going to be here for dinner. "Aye! Nat! Where you at?"

"I'm in the kitchen," she softly replied. The deeper I walked into the house, I smelled the food cooking. My stomach began to growl and ache. One thing about Nat, she could cook her ass off.

"What's going on? KJ said my moms coming to get him?" Nat's parents passed away so I knew he wasn't talking about them.

"Yeah, she is." She nodded as she stirred the pot.

"Okay, then what was the point of you texting me to come have dinner with KJ if she's coming?" I was a little irritated right about now. I could be cuddled under Niya's thick ass right now.

"I'm sorry, Kalib. It happened at the last minute. Your mom asked could she have him for the week, and I never deny her time with her only grandchild. Plus, I could use the break. Sorry for not telling you 'til now."

I noticed her voice was a little shaky, like she was about to cry or something. "Aye, Nat, what's wrong, ma?" I stepped into her personal space. Her hands were shaking while she was stirring the pot. Her head was down so it was hard for me to see her face.

She shook her head. "Nothing. I'm good, bro."

"Naw, you not. What's wrong, Nat?" I hated to see her cry.

Back when Kaleef first went to jail, she cried damn near every night. I was there for her most times. Sometimes I'd have to give her a bath and help change her clothes. She was that messed up behind Kaleef's arrest. Plus, she was pregnant.

Kanan would tell me that I was doing too much for her, but I never listened to his ass though. He didn't feel like it was our responsibility to take care of her, just KJ.

Nat being our big brother's wife, I was going to do all I could for her. I never told Kanan I'd seen her naked and shit from when I helped her bathe and dress. That nigga would act a damn fool and probably tell on my ass.

Kaleef wouldn't see the bigger picture. He'd put a hit out on me. I loved my big brother, but that nigga is ruthless.

"I'm fi—"

"Stop lying to me, Natalie!" I raised my voice at her.

Like clockwork, she started to tell me everything on her mind.

"Today is the day that Kaleef went to jail! I don't know. I guess I'm just emotional because it brings back so many memories, you know?

"KJ is going to be five soon, and Kaleef won't even be here to celebrate with us. I hate that my son hasn't met his father in person yet. He's heard his voice plenty, but the fact remains that KJ doesn't know Leef. He only knows you and Kanan.

"Lord knows when that nigga getting out of jail. He's so crazy he might've gotten more time added. He won't let me come visit him for shit. I mean, we're married. We can get a conjugal visit every once in a while! He doesn't even want to do that. Sometimes I feel like he's seeing someone else, like he's cheating on me in jail."

"Don't think like that, sis. It's going to be alright. Kaleef would never cheat on you. For one, he loves the hell out of you. You've held him down this long. Keep on holding him down. Two, you finer than a muthafucka. I know we fam and all but facts is facts, baby girl. My brother got to be dumb as hell or dropped the soap to give you up."

I was playfully biting my bottom lip at her and checking her out. I was only trying to get her to smile. It worked because she was smiling and giggling like crazy.

"Aww, you so sweet, Kalib. Sometimes I wish I met you first." She freely admitted, smiling and gazing into my eyes.

I stood there looking back. The truth of the matter was she did meet me first. She just wasn't interested in me back then. Kaleef was a rough neck and I was the calm one.

Females loved to underestimate me because I was quiet. They wanted Leef because he was outspoken, a little rude, and he could charm the panties off any woman he came in contact with.

He could have just called her a bitch and five minutes later she'd be undressing for him. He got that shit from our dad. Our dad was a charmer like Leef, quiet and observant like me, and could still cut up like Kanan.

"Kalib, did you hear me?" Nat brought me back to the present.

"Huh? No, what?"

"I said that you could go now if you want since KJ isn't going to be joining me for dinner—"

"Us," I corrected.

"Huh?" She appeared to be confused.

"You said me, as in just you. I'm saying us because I'm staying for dinner." I smiled.

She smiled back, not saying a word.

Just then I felt my phone vibrate in my pocket. I checked it and smiled when I saw Sexy's name across my screen.

Sexy: Hey, wyd?

Me: Having dinner with my sis. You?

Sexy: Getting ready to go out with Drea. Did you talk to Kanan yet?

Oh, shit! I had promised Niya I was going to talk some sense into K. Supposedly, he called their job going off on Niya about Drea. I had to go up in there and relieve Niya's stress and everything. She was taking her attitude out on me and I wasn't having that.

Me: Yeah Sexy I talked to him. He said he'll chill.

Sexy: Thank you boo! I don't know how I can repay you. This not my business but I love Drea like a sister. I can't have nobody doing her bad.

Me: No problem Sexy. Don't worry about it. I'll think of a bunch of ways you can pay me back. Lol!

Sexy: Bye nasty! Have a goodnight.

Me: Likewise Sexy.

I felt bad about lying but I didn't know what else to do. I only prayed K didn't go and do nothing dumb or else I'd be bailing his ass out of jail tonight.

Kanan

I was sitting across from Kalib's desk listening to him go on and on about me calling Aniya's work phone. All I wanted to do was get in touch with Andrea's clown ass. I'd been blowing her phone up, and she had the nerve to be ignoring me like I did some shit wrong. I felt like shorty was trying to play me so I took the car from her ass. I planned on giving it back but she kept ignoring me. I wasn't the type of nigga to take shit lightly. When I was pissed, everybody that was in my way was going to feel that shit.

"Man, yo' ass out here wilding, bro. Why would you buy her the car then take it back? Yo' ass an Indian giver," Kalib said while shaking his head. I started cracking up laughing because I hadn't heard nobody say that shit in a long time.

"Man, I was gonna give shawty the car back, but she ain't been answering the phone. That's why I called they work phone. Now I'm to the point where I want to go knock her fucking head off. I don't like when people ignore me. You out of all people know that."

"Man, fuck all that. Have you talked to Kaleef lately?"

"Naw, he ain't called me in a few weeks. That nigga probably in the hole or something. His ass ain't gon' ever get out, man. He keeps being a damn hothead."

"Yeah, I'm gonna take a trip to see him soon. His wife around here acting real crazy. She been crying a lot lately. I love sis, but I'm trying to put more of my time into Niya. You need to start going over there with her and KJ."

"I definitely will get my nephew, but I ain't trying to kick it with Nat. I told you, man, she ain't our responsibility."

"Nigga, that's Leef's wife which makes her family. When he get out and find out we ain't look out for her, he gonna kill both of us." I nodded my head because Kalib was right. Kaleef is a savage and I wasn't trying to go toe to toe with big bro.

"Alright, man, I'll hit her up in a few days. Maybe I'll take them to a game room or something. Little man loves playing basketball."

"Yeah, I installed him a basketball rim in they backyard the other day. He was happy as hell."

"Alright, bro. I'm about get up out of here."

"Where you going? We got work to do around here, man."

"I'll be back before they bring the new cars in. Don't worry, man, I'm on top of shit."

"Yeah, whatever, man. Just make sure you come back. I ain't trying to do all this shit by myself today."

"Bet." I dapped him up then walked out of his office.

I DECIDED to roll through Andrea's block to see if I would see her. It was a nice day out so I knew she was probably out with some hoe ass clothes on. I didn't know what it was about her but if she was any of the other chicks I fucked with I would have been left her alone. The first couple times I rode down her block I ain't see her. I decided to take one last spin around the block and when I pulled in her subdivision she was standing there talking to some clown ass nigga. I shook my head when I saw her in some little ass black shorts that had her ass hanging out. Then she had the nerve to have on a damn sports bra. I parked right in front of her complex so she could see me. I was riding in her car because I planned on giving it back if this conversation went well. I rolled the window down and she was just smiling and giggling in dude's face. The shit pissed me off so bad.

"Aye." They both turned and looked at me. When she saw it was me, she frowned her sexy ass face up then turned and started talking to dude again. "Drea, get in for a minute." I was trying to be calm with her ass.

"Hell naw, you got me fucked up. Take that car and ride the fuck off."

"Get in, Andrea." This was my second time speaking calmly to her, and I promised there wasn't going to be a third. She continued to stand there and talk to dude like I wasn't right there. I could tell dude was now feeling uncomfortable from the expression on his face. I swung the door open and hopped out the car. She tried to run but I grabbed her ass by the long ass weave she had in her head.

"Ahhhhhhh! Let me the fuck go, bitch!" she screamed as I drug her ass toward the car. I was now really pissed because she called me a bitch. That was the ultimate disrespect. She started punching me in the chest and digging her nails in my face. The shit hurt bad as fuck. I finally got a hold of both of her wrist and I hemmed her ass against the car.

"So I'm a bitch, huh?" She stood there breathing hard with her face balled up. See, this was the type of shit females liked. They liked to be roughed up and manhandled. *Damn, why she gotta be so fucking sexy?* She had the prettiest little face I'd ever seen. Even when I was mad at her I couldn't stay mad.

"Let me go, K! I'm done with yo' ass. Take this truck and shove it up yo' ass." I smiled at her because seeing her like this turned me on. She was so feisty and crazy. This was why I liked her. She didn't back down. I hated a female that couldn't handle me. You had to be able to tolerate my bad side and my soft side, and Andrea had proved she could handle all of my personalities.

"Give me a kiss."

"What? Hell naw, dude, get yo' ass off me." I still had her trapped against the car so she couldn't move. I was holding her wrist so tight that I was sure she would have bruises on them, but I didn't care.

"Who is that clown ass nigga behind me?"

"My man."

"I know you lying. I would never let another nigga be this close to my woman." I lowered my face and pressed my lips to hers. At first she didn't kiss me back but once I forced my tongue in her mouth she had no choice but to. I felt her body getting weak so I let her wrist go and wrapped my arms around her waist, lifting her off her feet. She threw her arms around my neck and let out a soft moan in my mouth. *Damn, I missed her crazy ass.* I broke our kiss and looked down at her with a big ass smile on my face. When I looked in her eyes, all I saw was lust. She was horny, and I was too.

"Yo' auntie in there?" She shook her head no. I massaged her ass and carried her towards her crib. I needed some pussy, and I couldn't wait any longer. I pushed the door open and Aniya was seating on the couch watching tv. I spoke to her but she didn't speak back. I guessed she was still mad about me calling her work phone. When Drea lead me to her bedroom, I slammed the door and instantly started snatching her little ass clothes off.

"Owww, K! Just pull my shorts down. You can't snatch these off, they're not panties."

"You could have fooled me. These muthafuckas look like panties. Don't wear these no damn more." I continued to take her clothes off and lick all down her neck. I was starting to figure out what turned her own. She went crazy when I stuck my tongue in her ear and sucked on her neck. I inserted my fingers inside her pussy and she was dripping wet.

"Oh, my god, K, please."

"Please what?" I was driving her crazy and I was doing it on purpose. The more I thought about the shit she pulled at the club, the more I wanted her to beg for my dick.

"Fuck me, Kanan."

"Tell me you sorry first."

"I'm sorry, Kanan. I'm soooo sorry." That was all I needed to hear. I threw shawty on the bed and got right to work.

IT HAD to be hours after I tore Drea's pussy up because when I opened my it was dark outside. We fell asleep after that make up sex. I looked around and I ain't see Drea's ass in the room. Her room was little as hell so I didn't have too many places to look. I heard voices in the front but I ain't want to just walk out there. I didn't know if her aunt was going to trip because I was here. When I heard my brother's voice, I hopped up and put my clothes on. When I walked into the living room, my brother, Drea, and Aniya were sitting in front of the tv laughing at some movie.

"You finally woke. I put that ass to sleep, huh?" Drea said, making Niya and my brother laugh.

"Yeah, whatever." I pulled her from the couch and sat her next to me on the loveseat.

"Bro, you know I needed you to come back to the dealership, but we gonna talk about that later." I ignored Kalib's ass because I didn't feel like arguing with him. We had hella employees so he didn't really need me.

"Bae, massage my feet." Aniya put her feet in Kalib's lap and he started rubbing her feet. Their asses were so cute it didn't make no sense.

"Bae, rub my feet." I put my feet on Drea and she pushed my shit away.

"Ewww, get those claws off me."

"I know my bitch love me 'cause she rub my feet," I rapped the lyrics to Black Younsta's song and we all laughed.

"On a serious note, we all need to do like a double date," Niya said while laying her head back and enjoying her foot rub.

"This is a double date," I said seriously.

"No, like a night out on the town."

"Yeah, that sounds cool, bae. I'm gonna see what I can make happen," Kalib said while kissing Niya's feet.

"Aye, bro, straight up, that's nasty as hell. Why would you kiss that girl feet?" I said while shaking my head.

"I've already kissed more than these feet," he said while winking at Niya. *Man, she got my bro head gone, and he ain't even hit yet.* I knew he didn't because he told me he hadn't.

ELEVEN

Andrea

I called myself trying to get out of this double date because I hated
skating. Kalib decided to rent out the whole skating rink so we all
could have a good time without a lot of people here. They invited a
few of their other friends, and everyone was skating, bowling, and
having a good time. I occupied the bar more than the skating rink
because I refused to embarrass myself. You would think since I grew
up in Georgia I would know how to skate, but nope! My ass only
went to the rink to find boys. While everyone else was skating, I was
trying to find a boyfriend. The skating rink was so bright and big. I
felt like I was in the movie ATL without all the people. All of their
friends were skating hand and hand with their ladies. I continued to
sip my drink and enjoy the beautiful scenery. I just had this feeling in
my body that everything was all good. I think I'm happy. That's really
rare for me, because my emotions are always up and down.

"So you gonna sit at the bar all night?" Kanan asked while sitting
in the barstool next to me. Looking at his sexy ass face was just a

breath of fresh air. Anytime I see him my pussy just throbs in all the right places.

"You damn right. I don't know how to skate, K," I wined.

"Come on, shawty. I'm gonna show yo' scary how to skate. Don't worry, I ain't gonna let yo' punk ass fall." He laughed while taking time to get skates. Kanan was a good skater. He even has his own pair of skates with his name stitched on them. Kalib had a similar pair with his name on them.

We were at the counter waiting for my skates when I noticed this pretty ass girl walking up to us. She was draped in jewels and designers and she smiled when she saw Kanan. *This better not be one of his bitches.*

"What's up, Kanan?"

"Hey, Nat. What you doing here? Where my nephew at?"

"He's with your mom. Kalib invited me to come out with y'all tonight. He told me I needed a night out."

"Aw, ok, that's cool. Nat, this is my lil' lady, Andrea. Andrea, this is my big brother's wife, Natalie," he introduced us.

"Hey, nice to meet you. You're one of the prettiest I've ever seen on Kanan's arm," Natalie complimented.

"Ohhh, girl, don't gas me up," I said while flipping my hair over my shoulder. We all laughed and walked over to the table where Kalib and Niya were sitting.

"What's up, sis? I thought you wasn't gonna make it," Kalib said while standing to hug Natalie.

"I'm here, Libby," Natalie said while wrapping her arms around Kalib. Maybe I was tripping, but that was not a sibling hug. I noticed Kalib tried to give her a church hug but she threw her arms around his neck. I mean, it is his brother's wife. Kalib introduced Niya then sat back down next to her, and Natalie sat on the left side of Kalib.

"Y'all having a good time?" Kalib asked while taking a bite of his chicken wing.

"Yeah, it's cool, bae. I haven't been skating in years." Niya looked so happy, and I was happy Kalib came and swept her off her feet.

"I haven't seen some of these people in years," Natalie announced while looking around at everyone.

"Yeah, I decided to invite everyone so we could have some fun. I ain't seen all the homies since the backyard party a couple months ago."

"You always the one to bring everyone together, Libby," Natalie said while putting her hand on Kalib's knee. *What the fuck is this bitch on right now?* I couldn't be the only one seeing this.

"Come on, bro. Let's go take a couple of shots real quick," Kalib said while standing and leading Kanan to the bar.

I took this as my opportunity to interrogate Natalie. Usually, when your brother brought a chick around to meet the family the sister was always grilling the girlfriend. In this case, I was asking all the damn questions because I smelled some fishy shit going on.

"So, Natalie, you pretty close to Kanan and Kalib, huh?" I asked my first question.

"Yeah, they're my brothers. They help take care of my son and I while my husband is in jail. Kalib has been a big help, and I can't thank him enough."

"That's what's up. So when does your husband come home? If you don't mind me asking."

"Hopefully, he'll home in a year or so. He says he might be out sooner because his behavior has gotten better and the prison is filling up so there's barley space. Only God knows though." She looked so sad when she talked about her husband. You could tell she'd been miserable without him.

"Well I hope he's home soon. There's nothing like being with the love of your life," Niya said while giving her a warm smile.

"How long have you and Kalib been seeing each other?" Natalie asked Aniya.

"Not that long. Almost two months."

"They so cute together. Don't you think so, Natalie?"

"Well I can say this might be the longest relationship Kalib's ever had. He hops from one hoe to the next. No offense, Niya."

"None taken, sweetie. I know who I am and Kalib and I are good. Excuse me, let me go and get my man." I stood up and followed Aniya to the bar where the guys were.

"What's up, shawty? You ready to learn how to skate?" Kanan asked while pulling me to the rink. I was scared out of my damn mind. I didn't want to fall and hurt my-damn-self. *I ain't got time to be sitting in the hospital.*

"Slow down, K."

"I'm not even going fast. Come on and let me just hold you. You ain't gotta do shit but put your arms around my neck, and I'll do all the work."

"But I'll be skating backwards."

"I got you, baby." I did what he said and surprisingly, I didn't feel scared. As long as he held me up, I'd be fine.

"You got pretty eyes, ma."

"Awwww, look at you getting all soft on me. You too cute, boy." Kanan blushed and shook his head.

"Here." Kanan pulled the keys to my car out of his pocket and gave them to me." I was hesitant, but I snatched them out of his hand anyway.

"You gonna take it back from me again?"

"Naw, it's yours. I promise. That was some bitch ass shit I did by taking it in the first place. I was just pissed off so I acted on anger and I apologize for that."

"I should have answered your calls and told you what I was doing. I ain't mean to make you feel stupid for getting me the car. I appreciate you a lot. No one has ever done anything like this for me." I kissed him on the lips, and for a second, I forgot there were other people there until I heard a loud scream. Kanan and I turned to see what was going on. Natalie fell on her ass in the middle of the rink and was being hella dramatic.

"Kalib, can you come and help me please? I think I twisted my ankle," Natalie's lying ass yelled to Kalib, and he skated his ass right to her like he was her puppy or something.

"Is she serious?" I asked Kanan.

"Man, Nat is always acting clumsy. And Lib always running to her damn rescue."

"I'll be right back." I skated slowly so I could make it back to the table without falling. Aniya was sitting at the table all in her phone. "Girl, what you doing in that phone?""Girl, posting a picture of Kalib and I on my Snapchat. We cute, right?" She showed me the picture and I agreed they were cute as hell.

"What you think about Natalie?"

"She's cool, I guess. I feel bad for her though. Her husband's been locked up for years and he's barley seen their child. It's fucked up."

"You don't think she's too dependent on Kalib? It look like she's being a little flirtatious if you ask me."

"Well I didn't ask you, Andrea. Why would you say that? That's his brother's wife for God's sake." I was confused why she was snapping on me. I was only trying to warn her.

"Niya, I could be wrong but look at them." I pointed to Kalib and Natalie. Kalib was on his knees, wrapping Natalie's unbroken ankle.

"He's helping her, Andrea. I swear you always try to bring out the bad in people." She stood and was about to skate off but I stopped her.

"Hey, I was only trying to help. If I see something suspect I always let you know. You're like my sister and I would never bring up any ole thing just to hurt you."

"I know, Andrea, but with this you're wrong. I'm not worried about Kalib doing anything like that."

"It's not Kalib I'm worried about either. It's that bitch Natalie. Just watch out for that bitch. That's all I'm saying, cousin."

"Alright, whatever." She skated off toward Kalib and rolled right into his arms. *Lord, I hope my cousin doesn't become one of these blind, dumb blonde ass girlfriends.*

"You ready to go?" Kanan snuck up behind me, scaring the shit out of me.

"Yeah, I'm getting tired. I think I had too much to drink."

"Let me get you home then. I like when you drunk," he said while rubbing on my booty.

"Boy, stop that shit."

I SAT on Kanan's bed angrily texting Darius' ass. He'd been blowing up my phone all damn week. I always turned my phone on do not disturb when I was with Kanan but for some reason I was still getting all of Darius' calls and texts. Apparently, the nigga thought we were in a relationship. How was that possible when I saw him with bitches all the damn time? I had to quickly text Darius before Kanan got out of the shower.

Me: Stop blowing up my damn phone like you my man or something!

Darius: Where the fuck you at man?

Me: What do you want Darius?

Darius: I got a lick for us. Meet up with me ASAP.

Me: I'll call you later. I'm busy right now.

I rolled my eyes then put Darius' ass on the block list. Darius and I used to hit licks all the time. We would do card cracking shit, fraudulent checks, and even set up niggas to be robbed. I hadn't done the shit in damn near three years so I was confused why he thought I was going to start that shit again. First of all, his greedy ass used to cheat me out my half of the money all the time. That was the main reason I stopped. Another reason was because I got locked up a couple times. After you see the inside of jail, I promise that shit would have you scared straight.

"Who the fuck you over there texting?" I jumped when I heard Kanan's voice.

"Nobody, just Niya asking if she can borrow on of my purses."

"Man, she's dating one of the richest niggas in town. She better tell bro to take her shopping."

"Aniya prides herself on being an independent woman. Besides, no matter how much shit a female has she always wants to borrow her cousin or sister's bag or shoes. That's what us women do."

"I guess. So what you about to do? I gotta go hang with my nephew for a few hours. You can come if you want."

"Where's his mama?" I ain't mean to sound harsh but the bitch Natalie was already acting flirty with Kalib. I didn't need her all in my man's face too.

"She said she gotta run some errands and shit, so I told Kalib I'll hold lil' man down."

"Aw, ok. Well go spend time with yo' phew phew. I'll meet him next time. I just wanna lay here and watch tv."

"Alright then. I'm gonna take yo' car because I don't want you sneaking off. I like seeing you in my bed when I come home." *This man knows how to make me blush, I swear.* I was liking him more and more every day. It was rare I found a guy I really liked. Kanan was a little rough around the edges but I could make it work.

TWELVE

Kalib
Sexy: I miss you. Wyd?
Me: I miss you too baby. I'm waiting to see Kaleef.
Sexy: Aww, okay. Well have a good visit.
Me: Thank you sexy. I hate being at this damn prison.
Me: When are you coming to spend the night with me?
Sexy: You're welcome...aww, you'll be aight. Just don't drop the soap! LOL!
Me: I see you got jokes though.
Sexy: Boy bye. Go see your brother.
Me: So you not even going to answer my question?

I watched my screen to see if she'd text me back, but I didn't see any signs that she was. She had me out here acting like a fiend. If I didn't talk to her one day, my whole day was off balance. That pissed me off and changed my mood. I was already irritated about being in this prison. I was always happy to see Leef, just not under these circumstances.

"Yeah, okay, Niya." I kissed my teeth, nodding to myself.

Niya had been avoiding coming to my house. I asked her a couple of weeks ago, but she just brushed it off like I didn't ask her anything. Niya did that shit often though. She only did it when we were having a serious moment. Anything else, she was cool about it. I was beginning to feel some type of way because I was opening up but she wasn't telling me much.

"Smile, nigga. What? You ain't happy to see your brother or something?" I turned around to see Leef standing there with open arms. After closing him into a brotherly hug, we took a seat across the table from each other.

"Wassup, bro? How you doing in here?" I braced myself for the answer. Leef hated whenever I asked him that but half the time I didn't know what to ask.

"Man, shit actually looking up for a nigga." He had a big grin on his face. That got my attention off Aniya for a hot minute.

"Oh, yeah? You ain't beat nobody up lately?" I joked. That got a laugh out of him.

He shook his head. "Nah, I been cooling it and keeping to myself. The sooner I get out of here, the sooner I can be under my wife and son."

I studied my brother, giving him the side-eye. This was a side of him I'd never seen before. I reached out and tried to touch his head with the back of my hand. He moved and swatted my hand away.

"Aye, nigga, chill. Don't tell me you switched teams since I been locked up." He was laughing but serious.

Now he had *me* messed up. "Hell nah. I'm eating pussy 'til I die. Shit, when I die, bury next to two bad bitches."

"Ayyye! That's what I'm talking about." He chuckled. "I'm just tired of being in here, Lib. I'll do whatever it takes to get out. I've came to my senses and it's not fair to Nat. You know her ass threatened to divorce my ass and leave with my son if I got put in the hole again?"

I had no idea. "Damn, when she tell you that shit?"

"Earlier this week she said that shit. You know I know Nat. She ain't playing with my ass. I'm already sick not being there for my son. I got to get my shit together before she leaves me for real."

"I guess sis ain't playing."

"Hell nah, she ain't." He shook his head. "I do want to thank you and K for stepping up and being there for lil' Leef. I owe y'all niggas."

"Nah, bro, we just doing our job as his uncles. Shit, it'd be the same energy if you were out. You and Nat would probably have a basketball team for K and I to spoil." We shared a laugh.

"Man, you ain't lying. I'm putting a baby in her soon as I get out," he confirmed with a lazy grin.

"I hear you, bro. Speaking of which...sis was crying about conjugal visits a few weeks back. I know you don't want her and KJ up here but maybe every two weeks break her off or something." I was only saying it because it messed me up to see and hear Nat crying. Personally, I felt like she was horny. Leef had been on lock for five years, so I knew she wasn't getting none.

"I hear you, man. Honestly, I don't want Nat up here or KJ. This is no place for them to be. Other than that, I don't want my son seeing me like this. Hell, I don't even want Nat seeing me like this. It's hard enough to see you niggas. You know I even told mama to stop coming?"

"That woman ain't hearing you, man." I waved him off with a laugh. My mama was going to do what she wanted. She always told us she was black, free, and proud. As long as she walked this earth, she was going where she pleased. Leef telling her not to come didn't mean shit.

"You already know she don't give a damn, bro."

"She ain't ever gave a damn about what we said. Remember pops told her don't be coming to the lounge because heavy shit be going down?"

"Hell yeah, I remember! Each and every time, ma went down there to get pops ass and brought him home."

"Man, we used to be rolling off that! Then pops try to whoop us for laughing."

"Man, I remember the first time he took me to the lounge. I was thirteen. Pops had just picked me up from basketball practice. Uncle Ben called pops going off because there was a fight that broke out so we went up there. By the time we got there, the shit died down. Pops said he was going to stay and have a drink. Man, I got my first lap dance right there and had my first drink."

"Damn, man, I ain't seen Uncle Ben since pops' funeral. You heard from him?" I knew if I hadn't heard from him, Leef probably didn't either. Still, I had to know.

"Yeah, he came by to visit me a few times."

That was news to me. "What did he want and why you never told K and me?"

"He didn't want nothing for real, just some of pops' old client information. I ain't tell y'all because him asking about some irrelevant shit was the furthest thing from my mind."

"Why would he want pops' old contacts? He should've already had the shit because him and pops ran together. Wasn't he supposed to be like his right hand or something like that?" I didn't know why I was getting so upset, but I was. I ain't never had a problem with Uncle Ben. He was always good people. He treated me and my brothers like blood, so he was good in my book.

Sometimes I did question why he didn't keep in contact with us after pops passed. Supposedly, him and pops grew up together and were best friends. If my best friend passed away, I'd make sure his family was good. Come to think of it, Uncle Ben disappeared right after my father's will was read. Pops left everything like his streets shit, businesses, and money to Kaleef, me and Kanan. He left my mama the house they shared along with everything in it and the cars.

"Aye, nigga, quit thinking so hard. I'll see you next visit." Leef stood from the table, holding his fist out for some dap. I was so wrapped into my own thoughts I didn't realize our time was up.

"Aight, bro, take it one step at a time." We embraced in a bro hug and parted ways.

On my way out the prison, I noticed my message icon had a five on it. I wasn't going to lie, my heart skipped a beat thinking it was Aniya. I was sadly mistaken. I had one message from my mom and four messages from Nat.

Ma Dukes: When you come to pick up KJ, bring me some chicken stock and fresh carrots.

Nat: Are you busy?

Nat: I need you to get KJ from your mom. I asked Kanan but he said he had something to do already.

Nat: I told your mom you'd pick him up.

Nat: I just want you to know how much I appreciate you, Libby! I swear me and KJ would be lost without you. LOL.

Picking KJ up wasn't in my original plans, but I didn't have a problem taking him home though. On the way to the store, I called my sexy to see what she was doing. After two rings, it went to voicemail. I hated that I was irritated about her not answering, but I was. It was out of my character to be doing all this back and forth, misreading shit. I was used to females throwing themselves at me. Then again, I had never wanted a woman as bad as I wanted Niya.

THIRTEEN

Niya

Once again, I was sending Kalib to voicemail. I'd been doing it for two weeks now. I hated that I was doing him like this, but I couldn't go any further with him. I was in my head about how fast things were going between us and I was starting to feel too dependent on him. I would wait around for his phone calls and texts. I would think about him all day, every day. I'd daydream about him and I would crave his touch. The shit was scaring me so I pulled away.

Lately, I doubled up on hours to keep myself occupied. It was just my luck too. The manager for night shifts was on vacation.

"Girl, I know you ain't going into work again tonight?" Drea asked as I walked downstairs dressed up for work.

"Nope, I'm going to the club with you," I joked, seeing what she had on. Drea was dressed in a strapless red dress with a deep V that stopped right under her small and perky breast. My cousin was looking like a whole meal right now.

"Girl, you not going to the club in that, unless you surprising

Kalib or something. Let me find out Kalib got you busting out your shell, being freaky." She giggled.

"Girl, why would I be trying to surprise Kalib? I'm about to go to work," I scoffed, heading toward the door.

"Bitch, you can't be serious right now," Drea snarled.

"Um, yes, I'm serious. Drea, you know I picked up Michelle shifts to get more hours. Why you acting brand new?"

"Niya, don't you know what today is?"

"Bitch, it's Friday. So what?" Usually, Friday ended our work week. Drea usually went out and I stayed in with mama. Since I picked up these hours, I'd been just working back to back.

"It's Kalib's birthday, girl!"

"What?"

Drea stared at me through narrow eyes. "The hell you mean, *what?* Didn't you know?"

"Drea, if I did, I wouldn't be on my way to work right now!"

"Why you working all these hours anyway? It's not like you hurting for the money. Plus, you work so hard in that damn office as is. What's going on with you, cuz?"

I shook my head, fidgeting in my stance. I never told Drea why I was truly picking up the extra hours. I told her I was helping our co-worker when that wasn't the whole truth. "Uhh, I'm just trying to make some extra money. I been thinking about moving out of here. We could get our own apartment, you know?"

"Bitch, if I move anywhere, it's going to be in a house and out the hood!"

"Well, yeah, I'm saving up for a house." I shrugged, trying to sell her that story. Drea wasn't stupid by far. She knew what I was doing, and I knew she knew.

"Mhm, you ain't —"

Knock, knock!

Thank, God! Saved by the door.

"Damn, you look good in that dress. I knew it'd look good on you." Kanan came in and kissed Drea on the lips. I stood back, watching them all boo'd up. A smile crept on my face. I was happy for my cousin. I could tell that Kanan truly made her happy.

"Wassup, sis?" Kanan came over and gave me a hug. "Girl, you not ready? Oh, you showing up on your own time? You gon' surprise bro, huh?" He chuckled.

"Yeah, I am. I just got home from work and forgot where he was having his birthday."

"Hold up, I thought you were —" Drea started to say until I cut her off.

"Yeah, I was but I changed my mind. So where is the place again?"

"Hold up, let me check my texts. Nat had everything set up and shit." Kanan put that snippet of information out there. I glanced at Drea who was staring me upside the head. Suddenly, she shook her head with a twisted face.

"Hold up, bae. Did you just say that *Nat* put the party together?" She added extra emphasis. Kanan's head snapped up from his phone.

"Yeah, she did. Why?"

"*Aniya* is Kalib's girl, not *Nat*," Drea spat. Kanan looked to me then looked away. I was standing there, not knowing how to feel. Truthfully, I didn't care who planned the party. I was more so upset with myself for not remembering Kalib's birthday. I picked the wrong time to cut him off. Now when I showed up to this party I was going in blind.

"Bae, let's go. Now," Kanan stated in finality. As bad as Drea wanted to put up a fight, she pressed her lips together and followed him to the door. K stopped at the front door before turning to me. "We going to Cooks and Soldiers, sis."

"Thanks." I pulled my phone out my pocket and went to Kalib's messages thread. There were so many texts from him over the weeks, and I'd only answered one message out of like the thirty messages he'd sent. I'd told him I was busy and couldn't talk. I didn't know why I did, but I held my breath as I texted him for the first time in two weeks.

Me: Happy Birthday!

WALKING INTO THE RESTAURANT, I felt so out of place. Not because of what I was wearing but because I would be seeing Kalib for the first time in what felt like forever. After coming up with a decent excuse why I couldn't make it in to work, I got started on my hair. Before, it was thrown up into a neat bun. I had decided to blow it out and straighten it. It had been a while since I wore my hair pressed so I forgot it was so long. Feeling the need to make a statement, I wore a clinging, white off the shoulder dress. I had plans of taking it back or giving it away but I never around to it. I felt like it showed too much cleavage and it was too tight on me. Then there was a slit starting at the middle of my thigh. Drea was always trying to get me in it, but I refused. To set the dress off, I added dark red lipstick, red Chanel six-inch stilettos, and the clutch to match. I had all this nice stuff but never wore it. One of my biggest excuses, we lived in the hood. If any of these hating hoes saw me with something nice, they'd plot on ways to be my friend or take what I had. I found out when I bought my car these hoes loved to hate and hated to see you with anything nice. The day I moved my mama and cousin out of the hood I'd feel so much better.

"Excuse me, miss. That's a private party. Your name has to be on the list." The waitress stopped me before I could walk toward the area everyone was in. No one could see me, but I could see them. My eyes instantly went over to Kalib. He had a half smile on his face and he looked high as hell. I gasped at how good he looked in his all white suit, red designer sneakers, and a red and white snapback that read 'Dope'. From where I was standing and he was sitting, I could tell he had gotten a fresh line-up and haircut.

"My name should be. It's Aniya Boles." I watched her check the list until she shook her head.

"No, ma'am, I don't see your name."

"This has to be some type of joke, right?"

"No, ma'am. Mrs. McClain told me to only let people who are on the list back there." I knew she was referring to Nat, so I didn't trip.

"Well could you go get Mrs. McClain, please?" I briefly smiled. I was trying my best not to act a damn fool in this nice restaurant. I felt a little slighted. Whether Kalib and I were talking or not, I should've been on the list. Now I was beginning to let my thoughts get the best of me. Kalib was being petty, I just knew it.

Noticing the waitress coming back with Nat in tow, I put a smile on my face. I wanted to get to the bottom of this in the nicest way possible. Nat's smile dropped when she noticed me standing there. It was as if she'd seen a ghost or something.

"Amaya, hey. I —"

"*Aniya*," I corrected. "Hello, Nat. I'm just wondering why I'm not on the list for Kalib's party."

"Umm, there is no easy way to say this, girl...but, umm, Libby said you weren't invited to his party." She offered a sincere smile. I tried, *tried* to smile back but hearing that I wasn't invited pissed me off.

"Is he for real?"

"Unfortunately, yeah." She nodded, this time without anyone emotion. "I mean, what did you expect? You haven't reached out to him in like a month. I'm sure you didn't think he would welcome you back with open arms so easily."

I was taken aback by Nat's response. It wasn't so much what she said but how she said it. It was like she knew something I didn't or something. I wanted so badly to slap the smug look off her face.

I took one step into her direction. "Look —"

"No, you look." She stepped all the way up to me. I noticed that Nat and I were the same height, even in stilettos. "You can't just come around here and treat Libby any ole kind of way. One minute you're all over him, got his nose wide open. The next you ignoring his calls and texts, treating him like a doormat. My son and I love that man very much and we don't like seeing him disappointed. If that's what you're going to do to him, stay away."

She didn't give me a chance to say anything. She just strutted back towards the party. I had so many feelings rushing through me at once. I knew for certain I wanted to slap the hell out of Nat. She didn't know me and she didn't know what was going on between Kalib and I. *That bitch better tread lightly.* Then again, she did have a point. Maybe it was best I stayed completely away from Kalib. I'd do him more harm than good.

FOURTEEN

We all were having a good time at Kalib's birthday dinner, but I couldn't help to think about Aniya. I kept looking at the door to see if I saw her.

"She coming, shawty. You know Aniya not gonna miss Kalib's birthday," Kanan whispered in my ear.

"I know, babe." I fixed the collar on his button up shirt and he smiled down at me like I was the best thing that ever happened to him. Looking around at the restaurant you could tell they paid a shit load of money to eat here tonight. You would think I would fee out of place being around all this money. Nope my ass feel right at home. I just can't wait until my cousin gets here so we can sneak diss.

"Y'all are made for each other," Natalie said, referring to Kanan and me.

"I hope so," I said while sipping my whine. Natalie kept trying to make conversation with me, but I wasn't here for it. I saw right through her bullshit.

"Bae, this shit good. Taste it. It tastes like fried chicken." Kanan tried to put the fried frog leg up to my mouth but I pushed it away.

"Ewww, stop it. I don't want that mess in my mouth."

"Aw, yeah? You want some other mess in yo' mouth, huh?" Both of our dirty mind having asses started dying laughing. This was what we did all day, every day. We talked shit, argued, and fought. This was why people said we were made for each other. I looked across the table at Kalib and he seemed to be having a good time, but I knew he wanted Niya to be here. I didn't know what was going on with Aniya because I barely saw her these days. The only time I got a good hi and bye was when we were at work.

"I'll be back, I gotta piss," Kanan said while hopping from his seat. I turned to look around the restaurant and I saw Natalie walking back toward us. I hadn't even noticed the bitch left the table. It looked like I saw my cousin walk toward the exit, but I wasn't too sure.

"Was that my cousin leaving?" I asked Natalie when she sat back down.

"And who is your cousin?" *This bitch really wants to play games with me today.*

"Aniya," I responded with an attitude. When I said Aniya's name, Kalib's head popped up from his phone.

"Aniya's here?" Kalib asked.

"I asked her if she was joining us. She peeked in then she said no and left out," Natalie said while digging into her food. I felt the bitch was lying so I hopped from my seat and ran outside to catch my cousin. When I got outside, she was just about to pull off.

"Niya, wait!" I screamed. I got in her passenger seat and when I looked at her face it was full of tears. "What's wrong, Niya? Why didn't you want to come in?"

"He doesn't want me there, and I don't blame him. I've been ignoring his calls and texts. I completely wrote him off and now he doesn't want to see me."

"Who told you he doesn't want to see you?"

"Natalie said he didn't put me on the guest list. She was saying all the shit I have been doing to him these past few weeks. It's like he told her all of our fucking business." The tears continued to slide down her face.

"First of all, I know for a fact that's a lie. She came and told us you peeked in then decided not to come in. I'm about to beat this lying ass bitch's ass." I hopped out of the car and stormed back into the restaurant.

"Bae, where you was at?" Kanan asked when I got back to the table.

"Bitch, I don't know what kind of sick game yo' ass playing, but you got her and me fucked up." I stood over Natalie with my finger pointed all in her face.

"Excuse you?"

"Why would you tell my cousin Kalib doesn't want her here?"

"You did what?" Kalib stood to his feet with anger written all over his face.

"I was just trying to protect you. You said you were upset with her and hurt. I didn't want it to ruin your birthday," Natalie said with a fake ass concerned look on her face.

"I confided in you because I had no one else to talk to, Natalie. Stay the fuck out my business. You don't make decisions when it comes to me and my girl. Fuck, man!" Kalib ran out of the restaurant and I was right behind him. When we got outside, he looked around for her car but she was gone.

"She's gone, Kalib. Just let her calm down a little then call her."

"Drea, I been calling and texting her for weeks now. What the fuck have I done wrong, man? She got another nigga or something? I'll kill his ass, whoever the fuck he is."

"It's not that, Kalib."

"Well what the fuck is it? I'm tired of playing these cat and mouse games with her. I'm too old for this shit. If she don't want to be with me, she needs to tell me. I can fall back all the way."

"If I knew I would tell you, bro, but I don't know what's up with her these days."

"I'm gone, man." Kalib walked to his car and sped away off.

"Where he going?" Kanan snuck up behind me. *He always doing that creepy shit.*

"I don't know. Let's go though, I ain't going back in there."

"WHAT THE FUCK the emergency about, Darius?" Darius and I were at IHOP in a low-key booth in the back. I finally decided to meet up with him and see what the hell he had been blowing my phone up about.

"I told you I got this sweet ass lick I want to hit."

"Naw, you know I don't do that shit any more. Find somebody else to help you."

"I can't."

"And why the hell not?"

"Because you fuck with the nigga I'm trying to hit up." Now this fool had me all the way confused. I dropped most niggas I used to fuck with because they got chump change. The only one I hadn't dropped was my sugar daddy.

"I don't have a nigga so you must be confused or bumped that big ass head of yours." He took his phone out and waved it in my face. It was a picture of me and Kanan. I swore my fucking heart instantly began to race. "Are you fucking crazy? Why the fuck you following me around? That's my man. I'm not helping you set him up."

"You and I both know you already have a plan on how to get in that nigga pockets." Darius was right. I did plan on getting nothing but money from Kanan, but I ended up falling in love instead. I never loved before so it was new for me. One thing was for sure, I would not set him up.

"Bye, Darius." I stood to leave, but he grabbed my wrist.

"Sit down. I'm not finish yet." I saw that dangerous, evil look in Darius's eyes and I sat back down. He pulled out a folder and sat it in front of me. "Open it," he instructed while eating his pancakes like shit was all good. I opened it and it was hella shit I had done. All my mug shots. Information on licks we hit and information about all the identity thefts I did. This folder of information would surely land my ass in prison for a long ass time.

"Darius, why are you doing this? You did most of this shit with me anyway."

"Did I? That's not what those papers and pictures say. Now what would happen if this ends up in the wrong hands? I just want to grab a couple of those foreign cars. Those are worth more than robbing him for some cash and jewelry."

"And how am I supposed to be of any use?"

"I know they transport their cars to and from their dealerships themselves. Just let me know the times and places."

"How? I don't have that information. They don't talk business around me."

"Figure it out. In the meantime, I'll hold on to this folder and give you time to figure this shit out." He grabbed the folder and walked out of the restaurant. His bitch ass didn't even leave money for the bill. *How the hell am I gonna set my man up to get robbed? What the fuck type of woman would I be?* Just when I thought I was done with that life, the shit came to bite me in the ass. *Maybe I should just tell Kanan and he and his brother can handle it.* What would he think of me once he saw all the things in that folder about me? He'll probably leave me and I know it. My aunt and Aniya always told me shit might come back on me ten times harder and they were right.

FIFTEEN

Natalie

"You have reached the voicemail box of...Kalib. Please leave a message after the tone."

"Hey, Libby, it's me...*again*. I'm sorry about last night. I didn't mean to hurt you. I was just looking out for you. Please call me back. I can't handle you being mad at me. You're all I got, you know? I love you."

This was my twelfth time calling Kalib. Every time I called he sent me to voicemail. Eventually, he turned his phone his off. Either that or he'd blocked my number from calling. I was no longer getting a dial tone, just his inbox.

"Mommy, can you call uncle Kanan and uncle Kalib over to play 2K with me?" KJ ran at full speed into the room. My heart always skipped a beat when I saw my baby. He was literally the main reason I was breathing. Kalib was the second.

I knew it was wrong, but I was in love with my husband's brother. I wasn't just talking when I told Kalib he was all I had. If it weren't for him, KJ wouldn't exist and I'd be dead.

When Kaleef went to jail, I wanted to die. We had just gotten married. We had our whole lives ahead of us, and he went and got arrested. I didn't sign up to be no 'ride or die' chick for a nigga in jail. I wanted to be a wife, a mother, and a lover to my husband.

I admit I was attracted to Kaleef's bad boy behavior at first. He knew how to have fun on his own terms and I loved that. Kalib said he was checking for me first, but I couldn't tell. He was remote and to himself. He acted like he was too good to speak at times. I wasn't offended because I wasn't interested in him.

It wasn't until recently when I found out how nice and sweet Kalib could be. He'd been here for me almost every day since Leef went to prison. There'd been plenty of times where I wanted to jump his bones, but I was too afraid. There's\d also been times I felt like he wanted me but he was too afraid of his brother.

Kaleef was three or more inches taller than Kalib. He was also more muscular than him. Kanan was the smallest out of the three. He had to be like five feet eleven, whereas Libby and Leef were in the six foot department.

"Yo?" Kanan answered the phone on the third ring. I didn't want to call his rude ass. However, for my baby, I'd do whatever he wanted.

"Hey, K. Your nephew wants you to come over and play 2K with him," I said in a sweet tone. I always tried to keep it short and sweet with Kanan. He could argue longer than anybody I knew. I wasn't here for it.

"I ain't coming there to play. Pack him a bag and he can spend the rest of the week with us."

See now he had me all the way bent. "Us? You know how I feel about my son being around people I don't know. You be having too many bitches around."

"I know this hoe ain't calling me a bitch, Kanan." I heard a familiar voice. "And what she mean, you be having too many bitches with you?"

"Bae, calm down. You the only bitch I got," he confirmed with a chuckle. Ole girl didn't find it funny because she was going off again.

"See, you about to get you and this hoe on the phone beat the fuck up! Keep playing with me. Who is this anyway?" she rudely inquired.

"Man, that's Nat. Give me my phone, girl, damn." I heard some shuffling in the back ground before Kanan got back on the line. "Yeah, Nat, we on our way. Have little man ready, aight?"

He didn't give me a chance to answer before he hung up in my face. I wanted to call back and tell him never mind, don't come but it was too late. KJ was right there and heard everything. He'd already taken off upstairs to get ready, I knew it.

Above all else, I would say Kanan was good to KJ and KJ loved his uncle. It wasn't Kanan I was worried about though. I didn't want KJ around this new heffa he had glued to his hip. I could tell she didn't mean him any good, not that I cared. Truthfully, I wouldn't be sad or surprised if this girl winded up using his ass and leaving.

SIXTEEN

Aniya

"This is the day, this is the day. That the Lord has made, that the Lord has made. I will rejoice, I will rejoice. And be glad in it and be glad in it! This is the day that the Lord has made! I will rejoice and be glad in it! This is the day, this is the day that the Lord has made!"

Sunday mornings were reserved for going to church with my mama. No matter how tired we were from the work week and weekend functions, Drea and I came to church. It was important to my mama. Plus, we got something out of it.

We'd been members at this church going on three years now. The last church we were at, the pastor passed away. They were going through too many transitions to get new leadership, so mama wanted to switch churches.

The church we attend now was cool and all. My mama adapted to it quickly. She was already teaching children's Sunday school and women's bible study on Tuesday nights.

"Girl, you ever notice pastor and auntie winking at each other?" Drea whispered in my ear as the song was ending.

I looked towards the pulpit at the pastor and then to the front pew at my mother. She sat in the front of the church with all the other mothers. "Girl, they not winking at each other."

I refused to believe my mama was being fresh. Then again, this was the same woman who told Kalib that she was next in line for one of his brothers. Speaking of Kalib, I missed him like crazy. Since he'd stopped calling and texting me, I figured he was done with me. I didn't blame him though. I caused this on myself. If I wasn't so caught up in my feelings, I'd be next to him right now.

"Yes, they did. You not paying attention because you either was into this song or thinking about Kalib."

"Kalib?"

"Yes, girl, Kalib, your man."

"Drea, he's not my man. He don't want me for real. I already told you what Natalie —"

"And I told you that bi—*female* played you!" She said a little too loud. I was thanking God the music was louder though. If anybody was listening hard enough, they'd hear Drea almost cursed in church. Us talking while service was carrying on was bad enough. If mama wasn't so into her praising, she'd cut her eyes at us.

"Drea —"

"Aniya, Kalib wants you, girl. He's just tired of you playing. You got that man confused and moody as hell. You need to just call that man and apologize."

As right as she was, I wasn't good at apologizing. It was a bad trait to have but I am who I am. Pray for me. "I guess."

"Girl—"

"I said praise the Lord, saints! I think sister Andrea has a testimony back there!" The deacon who was MC'ing the service called her out. Drea's face flushed light red and her eyes bucked as almost everyone in church turned to stare her down. I was praying Drea didn't start cussing everybody out.

"This nigga wanna be funny this morning," she spat under her breath, but I was able to hear. "Um, yes, Jesus is love." She stood to say then sat back down. After she said that, a few mothers and evangelists in the front took off dancing, my mama included. I wanted to laugh so bad, but I didn't want God to strike me down with lightening.

"Girl, just talk to Kalib." Drea went back to our conversation like nothing just happened. We were used to this by now, so it wasn't a big thing.

"Okay, I will." I sighed in defeat. *Lord knows I don't want to call this man.* I didn't even know what to say to begin .

Once offering was over and the choir went up to sing, I went to use the bathroom. As I stood in the stall against the wall, I stared at Kalib's name in my phone. *Girl, just call him and tell him how you feel.*

"I can't call him. He doesn't want to talk to me," I said out loud.

"How do you know he doesn't want to talk you? Did he say that?" I could've pissed my pants, hearing that deep and familiar voice. Smelling his cologne, I felt like I was about to faint. *I'm tweaking right now.* Yeah, that had to be it.

"God, let me get back into service before I be stuck in this bathroom," I said as I opened the bathroom stall.

"Damn, Sexy, you look good."

"Ahh!" I screamed, seeing Kalib standing against the sinks. "Jesus! Kalib, you scared me! What are you doing here?"

"I'm here to get a blessing. Aren't you?"

"That's not what I meant. What are you doing in the women's restroom?"

"I saw you headed this way so I followed you."

"You saw me? How? When did you get here? How long have you been watching me? Have you been stalking me?!" I had an uneasy feeling settling in my loins. Kalib being here wasn't sitting right with me. Then it hit me. "Did Drea tell you where I was or something?"

"Calm down, ma. I haven't been stalking you. No, Drea didn't put me up to this. I just remembered you telling me that you came to church with ma every Sunday. You don't remember telling the name of the church and inviting me?"

I stood there jogging my memory. Over the two months Kalib and I'd been talking, we've shared a lot of information. Well, he had anyway. He was always trying to get me to talk about my past and 'open up'. I'd swerve him each time though.

"Yeah, I guess I did." I shrugged, moving past him to wash my hands.

"So that's all you have to say?" He sounded like he had an attitude. I looked at him through the mirror and shrugged.

"What do you want me to say, Kalib?"

"How about you start with why you've been pulling away from me, Aniya? What did I do?"

"You didn't do anything. It's not you, it's—"

"Awl, naw, don't give me that bull, man. I want the truth, Niya. One minute we good and everything is lovely. The next you ignoring my calls and texts without explanation."

"I...I-I umm—"

"Can you just be real with me? If you don't want me, I'll leave you alone. I promise you I will."

Hearing him say that made me feel like I was losing the air out my body. "No, I promise I want you. I just...I just don't think I'm good for you." Finally saying the truth, I let go of the imaginary breath I'd been holding in. Lord knew I wanted Kalib so bad. It was just a part of me felt like I didn't deserve him or he didn't want me. Even with the signs that he did slapping me in the face, I felt this way.

"What? Niya, I been showing you every day I want you. I don't believe that for a second. You got to know I want you. It's something deeper you're not telling me. I keep trying to get you to talk to me, but it's like pulling teeth. I can't and won't force it out of you, but, baby girl, you got to let that shit go if you want our relationship to go further."

Why did I feel like those were parting words? Like he was saying goodbye to me? Kalib stood there for a few more minutes, staring at me, waiting for me to say something. It was like he just knew after saying that, I'd start spilling my feelings. As desperately as I wanted to, I couldn't do that. I wasn't ready.

"Take care of yourself, ma. You know where to find me when you ready." He kissed my forehead and walked out the bathroom.

SEVENTEEN

Kanan

Ever since Aniya and Kalib broke up, Niya had been like a third wheel. She'd do movie night with us, date night with us, and she even shopped with us. I was starting to feel like I had two bitches. All I wanted was for Drea and I to have some alone time, but Drea took it upon herself to invite Aniya with us to this art show one of my favorite tattoo artist was putting on. He threw this event once a year, and Kalib and I always showed our faces. Kalib must have changed his mind about coming because we'd been here for at least an hour and he hadn't arrived yet. I ain't tell him Aniya was coming because I ain't know her ass was tagging along. Don't get me wrong, I fucked with sis, but she'd been third wheeling too much.

"Hey, this is a nice piece. What y'all think of this?" Niya asked Drea and I.

"Yeah, that shit slick. I wonder how much it is," Drea responded like she had a big ass house to hang that big ass painting.

"And where you plan on hanging that at? Not in yo' lil' ass room." I started cracking up because the shit was funny.

"Aw, you got jokes, huh? I'll hang it in yo' damn house." Drea looked down at her phone for the hundredth time tonight. Her ass had been acting weird lately. I couldn't put my finger on it but what was done in the dark always came to the light.

"I'm gonna go to the bar. Y'all want something?"

"We'll take champagne," Niya answered for them. Drea was too busy texting on her phone to answer me. I walked to the bar and ordered our drinks. I wanted to get Drea drunk tonight so we could have some fun alone time.

"What's good, bro?" I turned around and saw my brother, and Natalie was standing right next to him. I could have sworn he wasn't talking to her after what she did at his dinner party.

"What's up, man? What she doing here?" I asked pointing to Natalie.

"I always come to the art show," Natalie said with a stanking ass attitude. This bitch had really been pissing me off lately.

"I thought y'all two weren't speaking to each other."

"At the end of the day, this sis. We gotta look out for each other. She was only looking out for me but I didn't appreciate it at the time." *Man, this nigga gotta be fucking kidding me.*

"Man, she did that shit to fuck up what you got going on with Aniya. Don't be blind to her bullshit," I spoke like the bitch wasn't even standing in front of us. Natalie had been on some other shit and I didn't like it.

"Excuse you?"

"Bitch, you heard me." At this point, I didn't give a fuck whose wife she was. The bitch wasn't been acting like a wife.

"Aye, chill out, K. Apologize to her now," Kalib had the nerve to tell me to say. He knew that shit wasn't happening.

"Fuck out my way." I bumped past them and went to find my girl.

"You see Drea, Kanan? I think I'm about to leave," Aniya asked with a scowl on her face as she looked toward Kalib and Natalie's direction. Kalib and Aniya looked at each other intensely from across the room. I could tell Aniya was hurt, but it wasn't my business so I was going to stay out of it.

"Come on, I'm gonna take you home."

AFTER DRIVING ALL the way to Aniya and Andrea's crib to drop Aniya home, I was tired as hell. There was no way in hell I was going to drive all the way across town to my crib, so we decided to stay at her crib for the night. I liked staying at Drea's crib because her aunt was mad cool and she always made breakfast, lunch, and dinner. I'd been thinking about introducing Drea to my mom. I didn't think she would go for it because she was so used to not being in a relationship that she thought I didn't want us to be exclusive. I'd never fell for a chick so fast and I definitely wanted this forever.

"Bae, how you feel about meeting my moms?"

"What? Boy, cut it out." She broke out in laughter like it was a joke.

"What's funny? I'm dead ass serious. Moms been trying to figure out who the chick that's been taking up all my time."

"You know I don't do meet and greets."

"What's the fucking big deal, Andrea? If your moms was here, I would want to meet her." I knew talking about her mom was a sensitive subject, but she needed to know this shit was important to me. *Hell, she should be lucky I want my moms to meet her ass.*

"Well my mom ain't here so let's not go there." She got up from the bed and started messing with shit on her dresser.

"I'm just trying to make shit all the way official with us. Ain't that what females like? Hell, I don't know. I'm just trying to make you happy, Andrea." *She got me acting like a soft ass nigga right now.*

"Well maybe I don't want that. Maybe I'm happy with just being friends with you." I almost slipped up and slapped the shit out of her for letting that bullshit fly out her mouth. *Ain't no friends, bitch.*

"Man, get the fuck on with that bullshit you talking. We been kicking it all this time, I take yo' ass shopping damn near every day, bought yo' ungrateful ass a whole fucking car and now you want to sit up and yell some friend shit to me?" She had me up on my feet, pacing back and forth. This was something I did to prevent myself from knocking motherfuckers out.

"Calm down before you wake my aunt."

"I will wake this whole fucking block! I don't give a fuck! You must got another nigga or something. You been acting real strange lately. Running in the bathroom to use the phone and shit. Matter of fact, where the fuck yo' phone at? You got me fucked up, shawty. Yo' ass probably fucking with every broke ass nigga in Georgia and I don't know." I started ripping her room apart to find her phone. Her ass was always on her phone but I hadn't seen it since we got in. *She had to hide the shit.*

"Kanan, stop it!" she yelled, but I kept on snatching shit out her dressers. I was determined to find that motherfucking phone. I noticed that Andrea stopped yelling, so I turned around and saw she was sitting on the floor with a face full of tears.

"Fuck is you crying for? Don't cry now." I noticed she was holding something in her hand. I looked closer and it was a ripped photo of a little girl and a lady. I assumed it was her and her mom. *Damn, did I rip that?*

"Get out," she spoke so softly and calmly it scared me.

"Baby, I'm sorry. I didn't mean to rip it. Come here, let me fix it." I tried to reach out to her, but she went crazy on my ass. She was punching and scratching me, and I just stood there and let her.

"Get the fuck out nooowwww! I hate you."

"What's going on in here?" Her aunt and Aniya rushed in the room, damn near breaking the door down. They saw Drea crying with the ripped picture in her hand and they ran to her side.

"Just go, Kanan. She'll be fine, don't worry," Aniya said while hugging Drea. I did what she said and just left. I knew she wasn't going to want to speak to me and this would be an excuse to leave me. Me and Drea had been straight so I didn't know why she had such a sudden change of heart. *I'm gonna let her breathe for a couple of days then reach out.* Hopefully, she reached out before then.

EIGHTEEN

Andrea

I didn't know why I broke down like that when I saw Kanan's dumb ass ripped the picture of me and my mom. That was the only good picture I had of the two of us when she was clean. I rarely looked at the picture because it made me emotional. Kanan's ass really wanted to find my damn phone. *He's dumb as hell because my phone was underneath my damn pillow.* I should have just told him I would meet his mom. I'd been low-key trying to distance myself from him. I felt if I distanced myself from him then Darius would change his mind about this whole robbery situation. *Who am I kidding? Darius found the golden ticket and he ain't gonna stop until he cashes out.*

"Hey, you ok?" Niya asked while picking up all the shit Kanan knocked off my dresser.

"Yeah, I'm good. He's a fucking clown. I'm done with his ass."

"No, you're not. Couples get in arguments, Drea. Who gets mad because a man wants you to meet his mom? You know that's a good thing, right?"

"I don't care about none of that shit, Niya."

"What do you care about then, Andrea? The picture? We have lots of pictures of your mom."

"Not like this though. It's fine though, I'll be fine like always."

"You sure?"

"Yup, you know me." I was good for putting things in the back of my mind. I didn't have time to cry and be sad about shit I couldn't control.

"Mother's Day is coming up soon. Maybe we should go to her grave and put flowers and balloons on her headstone," Aniya suggested.

"Aniya, she doesn't have a headstone, remember?" We couldn't afford to get my mom a headstone when she passed away. My aunt always lived check to check and barely could afford everything we wanted and needed.

"Aw, yeah, I forgot. Sorry, cousin."

"We need to go clubbing. We haven't been out in so damn long. We both single, bitch."

"Girl, you better stop saying you single before Kanan beat yo' ass."

"Girl. I'm not thinking about his stupid ass. All I want is a big ass glass of liquor and some good music. That's the only thing that's on my damn mind. If you don't go with me, I'll find somebody else to go, bitch."

"Where you trying to go? I can admit I deserve a night out. I haven't been to a club in so damn long."

"So get ready, bitch. We about to go shake some ass."

"Aw, you talking about right now?"

"Yea, bitch." I opened my closet door and got to looking through all the shit Kanan bought me. *Damn, man, it's crazy how spoiled that man got me.* All I had to say was "baby, I want this or that" and that man would run and get it for me. He was really a good dude and I definitely didn't want to lose him. I needed to just tell him about Darius, but I was scared as shit. I was pissed at how he acted tonight, but that was little shit. I'd let him sit and think about what he did for a few days.

"Damn, that's cute, girl. Can I wear that?" Aniya snatched the all black Versace body con dress out of my closet so fast it hit me in the damn face.

"You can have it, girl. You gonna be snatched in that dress."

"I have the perfect shoes for it, girl. Hell yeah, honey! Let me go get ready." Aniya ran out of my room like a kid in a candy store. She was actually happy to go to the club with me. I needed to hurry up before she changed her damn mind.

WHEN WE WALKED in Magic City, it was so damn live. I felt like I was right at home. I hadn't been clubbing since Kanan called himself popping up on me at the club a couple months ago. He told me I could only go to the club with him. *I swear that man thinks he's my daddy.*

"Oh, my goodness. Look at all these whores. They should be ashamed. In here shaking ass for dollars," Aniya said with her nose turned up. *I swear I can't take this bitch no-damn-where.*

"Come on, I got us a private section. I knew yo' ass wasn't gonna want to stand around with all the regular folk."

"They got Vodka? I don't want any dark liquor tonight. That dark shit have me hung over. Remember we still have to work in the morning."

"Damn, I forgot all about work. I do not want to walk in that place." We walked through the crowd to our section and we barely made it without me cussing thirsty ass niggas out.

"Damn, I forgot how thirsty dudes be for a fine ass chick," Aniya said while flopping down on the couch.

"And we looking extra fine tonight, cousin." Aniya was rocking the black Versace dress that stopped in the middle of her thighs and a pair of nude heels with her hair pulled back in a ponytail. I was rocking some skintight jeans with a white halter top and red Giuseppe heels.

"Come on, girl, let's drink." Aniya poured herself a glass of Cîroc and I poured me a glass of Henny of course. I waved over a couple of dancers and handed Aniya a stack of ones. "Really, Drea?" I laughed because I knew Aniya don't like strippers dancing on her.

"Have fun, girl, damn." Aniya started throwing the dollars on the strippers like an amateur. "This is how you do it, bitch. You gotta make it rain." I stood on the couch and started throwing money all over them. They were shaking ass like this was the last time they would ever do it. Niya stood up and followed suit.

Everything I was going through instantly went to the back of my mind. Listening to this music and dancing really help me escape life for a moment. Being with my cousin really brought a sense of calmness to me and I felt right at home with her being next to me. The club was full of drunk ass people but who cares.

NINETEEN

Kaleef

Being a free man was something I never thought would come true for me. My ass could have been free a long time ago if I didn't beat so many niggas ass in there. Being a McClain brother came with a price. Everyone knew our family and police always targeted us because of who our father was. I'm hothead, I could admit that. I wasn't going to ever let a motherfucka test my gangster. Right or wrong, I handled my shit. Since my brothers and I didn't choose to take over my dad's empire, niggas thought we were bitches. They quickly found out we were the opposite of that. Me being the oldest, I always took more heat and made sure my brothers were good. I always had to keep an extra out on Kanan because he was the youngest and his temper was almost as bad as mine, maybe even worse.

When I found out I was getting out early due to the prison being overcrowded, I was happy as hell. I called my homie first because I wanted to surprise my family. I knew Natalie was going to be emotional and happy as fuck. *I swear I can't wait to see KJ.* I hadn't seen my son at all. I know that lil; nigga looked just like me. I couldn't wait to spoil him, play ball, and all that other extra shit fathers did. The first thing I was doing when I saw Nat was taking her ass in the bedroom. I wasn't trying to hear no talking. I had to beat my meat for years thinking about her but now I could have the real thing. We could have did those lil' marriage visits, but I ain't want my wife nowhere near that prison. I knew it upset her but at the time I thought it was smart. One day I hoped she'd forgive me for putting our family through this bullshit.

"Damn, nigga, I'm happy to see yo' nappy head ass," My homie Rich said while driving. He picked me up and took me to his crib to shower and put some new clothes on. I didn't want to pull up on my family looking a damn mess.

"Man, you don't even understand how happy I am. I'm ready to crawl up in my wife's pussy. Put a hurting on shawty's ass, man." We both laughed. I noticed he wasn't going in the direction of my house. I knew I'd been locked up for a minute but I also knew Georgia like the back of my damn hand. "Where we going, man? It's getting a little late, I want to see my people."

"Man, you can spare a few more minutes with ya boy. You gonna be tide to yo' family for a while so let's gone head and enjoy this night, homie."

"You right."

"Here, nigga, you gonna need this." He tossed me a box and it was an iPhone.

"How the fuck am I supposed to set this shit up?" I took the phone out the box and started playing around with the phone.

"Don't worry, yo' son will teach you. Kids good with phones and shit." I laughed at the thought of my lil' son showing my old ass how to use a phone. When we pulled up to the strip club, my eyes were wide open. I hadn't seen women in so long my ass almost hopped out the car while he was still driving.

"This why you had a nigga hop fresh and shit? Yo' barber hooked my head up though. I like this lil' sponge look." He pulled up to the front of the club and valet came and opened our doors. This was something I missed. The whole V.I.P treatment shit. We hopped out the car and went through the side entrance of the club. When we got in the club, it was like a dream I swear. It was ass and sexy women everywhere.

"Like heaven, right?" I had a big ass Kool-Aid smile on my damn face. Two seconds later a crowd of bad bitches circled us with big bottles of liquor. They led us to the stage so we could have front row action. One of the ladies poured me a glass of liquor and everything was a blur after that. We were taking shots to the head like crazy. I hadn't had a drink in years so I was taking it all in. Bitches were dancing all on me and my dick was rock hard. Those hoes were trying to take me to the back but I wasn't going for that shit. The only pussy I wanted tonight was my wife's. When I looked over at Rich, his ass was drunker than me.

Aye, nigga, where yo' car keys at? You ain't driving me home. I just got out and I'm trying to make home to my family, man."

"Man, yo' ass don't know how to drive. Valet got my keys anyway," Rich slurred over his words.

"You forgot I own a damn dealership? I can handle my liquor better than you, lil' nigga." We walked through the club and out the side entrance. The car was there waiting for us when we got out, and I rushed to the driver side before Rich could.

"Man, so you really gonna drive? Let me put my seat belt on. You ain't drove in years, man."

"So!" I got in and put the car in drive. As soon as I put my foot on the gas, I hit the truck in front of me. It was a nice ass truck too. Two sexy ass women hopped out yelling and screaming, being dramatic as fuck.

"See, nigga, I told you yo' ass can't drive." We hopped out the car and the girls were walking up on us looking mean as shit.

"You ain't see us right in front of you? You blind or something? 'Cause if you is, you should not be driving." I couldn't do shit but laugh because this fine ass woman in this tight black dress was sexy and feisty as fuck. Her eyes were low and red, so I knew she was drunk as shit just like me.

"My bad, sweetheart. I ain't mean to fuck yo' truck up." I grabbed her hand and leaned to kiss the back of it, but she snatched away.

"Ewww, I don't know where yo' lips been. It's not my truck, it's hers and her man gonna be pissed the fuck off."

"Calm down, Aniya, it's fine. He'll get it fixed. And I wish he would act crazy with me again after the shit he pulled with me. He owes me so I'm not worried. Besides, it's not that bad."

"Yeah, whatever, Drea. Give us your information for the insurance company. And your cell number too. Just in case you try some funny shit."

"I don't know my cell number," I told her while looking at her titties. She had her shit all out on display, so I couldn't help myself. I took my phone out my pocket and she snatched it out my hand.

"How the hell you don't know your own number? Here, I called my phone off yours so you'll know it's me calling about the insurance."

"That's all you need me to call for?" I flirted. The shit just came out. I didn't know why I was flirting when I'd just got out and was about to go surprise my wife.

"Whatever, perv." I laughed because I thought she ain't catch me looking at her titties, but I guessed she did. I watched as they hopped back into the truck and pulled off. *Damn, it's good to be out.*

TWENTY

Kalib

Man, I didn't know how I let it get so late and I was still at Nat's house. After the tattoo show, we came right back to her house. I planned on leaving right away, but she wanted to sit and talk a little. She kept on apologizing about what she did. Honestly, I was over it. I learned a long time ago not to hold grudges. At the end of the day, Nat was my sis and she had my nephew. I wasn't about to let my feelings over Niya come between that.

Oh, damn. I checked my phone and noticed it was close to four in the morning. Me and Nat had literally just been up, sitting on the couch and talking while sipping pink Moscato. I wasn't usually a wine type of nigga but I'd admit the shit was good.

"Aye, sis, I better get going. I got to be at the dealership in like three hours." Most people who owned businesses liked to hire people to run their companies. That wasn't me. I liked to be hands on so I knew the job was getting done. My favorite thing was when we had difficult customers. They'd ask where the manager was and I'd laugh before telling them I was the owner. The responses were always priceless. There were plenty of dealerships in Atlanta they could go to. They wanted to get serviced by McClains because we treated our customers like family.

"Libby, don't go," Nat whined. I didn't know if it was the wine or what, but Nat was looking and sounding all innocent.

"Nat —"

"Libby, it's late. How about you sleep in the guest bedroom? KJ will be back later in the day. I could make us breakfast?"

"Nat, I don't know, sis. I really should —"

"Kalib McClain, you're staying here and that's final."

"Damn, you my mama now?" I smirked. As soon as I stood to get up, I fell back down. "I know that fruity shit ain't got me tipsy. Nat, I only had two glasses."

"Nigga, you had two *full* glasses of that *fruity shit*, as you call it." She giggled. After sitting for a few more seconds, I stood again. I was a little lightheaded but able to stand. "Here, let me help you, boo."

Nat came over and placed her arm around my waist and walked with me through the house. When we got to the guest room, she helped me take off my shirt. I didn't ask her to do that, but I wasn't stopping her. Next she reached for my belt to pull my pants off. This reminded me of the times I would help her get dressed and undressed.

I started to feel some type of way about her doing this and pushed her hands away. "It's okay, sis. I got it now. Go to bed."

She reached her hands out to touch my belt again. This time when I pushed her hands away she had a strong grip on my pants.

"Nat, what you doing? I said I got it."

"I know but let me help you." She stared intensely at me. I tried to read the look dancing in her eyes but they captured me as she continued to help. Slowly, she squatted and my eyes followed her. She was untying my shoes now. In a swift motion, she yanked my boxers down and grabbed my dick in her small hands.

"Whoa! Nat...shit...the fuck is you doing?" She didn't give me time to pull away before she was going to work on me. Grabbing her by the back of her head, I wrapped my hands in her hair. I was about to ease her off me 'cause this shit wasn't right. *But why it feel so good?* I was stuck—literally. Who knew Nat was this good at giving head?

"Fuck, girl, why you doing this?" I knew my ass was sounding like Jody off *Baby Boy* when ole girl was sucking him up.

"Mmm!" Nat shoved me all the way down her throat, chocking on my dick. I won't lie like I wasn't loving the feeling of her throat massaging my third leg. In my mind, I was telling myself how foul this was. I wished my body would react the same way.

"Shit, I'm about to bust!" I took over and fucked her mouth to finish me off. At that point, I was like 'fuck it'.

"Ooohhh, Kalib! I knew you'd be so big and feel so good inside me!" Nat was now fully naked and riding my dick like a cow girl determined to stay on a bull. Once again, I had to tell the truth. Nat had some good and tight pussy.

I had one handful of her ass and another handful of her hair. Nat was matching every stroke I threw her way.

"Shit, ma." I hissed, feeling her squeeze her tight pussy around me like a vice grip. "Just like that!"

"Like that, baby?" She popped her ass the way I told her.
Smack!

"Just like that, ma." I bit my bottom lip to concentrate on getting both of us where we wanted to be. I didn't know the stress I had pent inside 'til now. I knew she had plenty of stress and freaky shit going on in her mind.

"Ooooh, Kalib, I'm about to cuuum!" She rode me faster. I looked down and noticed her toes were curling and she had a death grip on her nipples. If she pinched them any harder, she might pop them.

"Cum for me, Nat." I got out between breaths. I was about to bust too.

"Kaliiiiib! I'm cumming, baby! Cum with me!" She went crazy, bouncing on my dick and squirted all over my lap. I swear that was the sexiest shit I'd ever seen. I felt myself rock up then my nut built and felt like I was about to erupt like a volcano. Nat slammed down one good time and bent over to touch her ankles while still on my dick. I couldn't take it no more. I let my seed go all up in her guts.

A few minutes passed and we both caught our breaths. There was now an uncomfortable silence between us. It was like the atmosphere was yelling, 'you know you fucked up, right?'

"Fuck was that about, Nat?" I calmly asked. I wanted to be mad at her and point the blame. I couldn't though. We both did this. I should've stopped her the minute she was helping me undress.

"I was tired of holding back, Libby." Nat exhaled. It was like she'd been holding that breath in forever. The funny thing, she didn't sound like she was sorry it happened.

Me on the other hand, I wished it was under different circumstance. Like maybe if she wasn't married to my brother and have his kid I'd feel okay about it. "This can't happen again, Nat, and Leef can never know. You do know that, right?"

"Fuck him!" She sat up on the bed. "I'm done with his as anyway. I want you, Libby."

"The fuck do you mean, *fuck him?* That's my brother, Natalie!"

"Just like I said, Kalib, fuck him! He's been saying that to me for five years! I'm over it. I want to be happy and I want you."

"Ma, you ain't thinking straight right now. You saying you want to leave my brother for me? A nigga you married to and got a whole kid with!" Now I was getting irritated. I could see Nat didn't care no more. None of this was in her character at all.

"I'm divorcing him. I already filed the papers and sent them to the prison. You can stop looking at me crazy, too. I don't care what anyone says or thinks. I deserve to be happy with who I want to be happy with." She walked up on me and caressed my face, but I moved out of her grasp.

"I'm sorry but that person isn't me, Nat." I shook my head at her solemnly.

"Who is it then? Huh? That Aniya chick? She doesn't want you, Kalib, I do! Can't you see that?"

Even though what she was saying about Niya might've been

somewhat true, I didn't want to hear the shit out loud. It was like she was pouring salt into my open wound. Nat knew how I felt about the way Aniya was treating me. "Bye, Nat."

Quickly, I snatched my boxers and jeans and walked out the room. I managed to get majority of my clothes back on as I was rushing down the stairs. Nat came running after me in a robe. She was crying with her makeup running.

"Kalib, please don't leave. I want you—" she stopped talking mid-sentence. Her body began to shake and she kept opening and closing her mouth. It was like she'd seen a ghost. "Ka-Kal-l-leef?"

"Huh?" I asked in confusion and she pointed behind me. I turned and followed the direction of her finger. Sure enough, it was my brother standing there in the flesh. *When this nigga get out?*

Kaleef

One...two...three...four...five...six... I continued to silently count to myself. This was something I'd learned in prison therapy. Counting one through ten helped you make better decisions and choose your battles. Getting to five meant you're good and in control of yourself. Getting to nine meant you'd been tested and showed your opponent what was really good. I'd just made it to ten. Ten meant you couldn't handle the situation in an accepted manner and reacted to destroy. You could imagine how I felt when I walked into my home and saw my brother and my wife running down the stairs half naked.

"K-ka-leef, what you doing home, man?" Kalib had his hands up, protecting his face the whole time he tried to get my name out.

"Why the fuck you got yo' hands up, lil' nigga?" This was something I always asked my little brothers when they were younger. Before I even asked them anything, they would raise their hands in defense because they knew I would knock their asses out for lying. I knew he was about to tell me a lie so I knocked his ass out before he could think of one.

"Kaleef, what are you doing? Stop it!" I continued to stomp the shit out of Kalib while Natalie tried to pull me off him. She hopped on my back and bit my damn shoulder.

"Awwww, bitch, get the fuck off of me!" I back slapped the shit out of Natalie, sending her crashing to the floor. At this point, I wanted both of them dead. After getting tired of stomping his ass, I stopped and stood over their asses. I swear I was glad I wasn't strapped because only the lord knows what would have happened. Kalib laid there growling while covered in blood. "Both of y'all dead to me." I walked back out the house, and luckily, Rich was still sitting back in his car sleep. I hopped in and drove to my mother's house.

As I drove to my moms' crib, so many thoughts ran through my mind. *How long have they been fucking behind my back? Why would my brother do me like that? Why would my wife do me like that?* I wanted to turn around and ask them all these questions, but I knew I would start beating his ass again. All this time I put trust into my brothers and look what the fuck happened. Blood didn't mean shit. It was niggas out here that had been loyal and weren't even blood. Like Rich. Rich made sure he sent me money when I didn't need it. He visited at least once a month. This nigga was more of a brother than my own. I was so damn pissed I ain't even notice I had tears falling down my face. I felt like a bitch, crying and shit. That was my wife though. I protected her, I loved her. I did every fucking thing for that bitch. I even married her ass when everyone was telling me not to marry that gold digging bitch.

When I pulled up to my mother's crib, I was exhausted. I didn't even want to get out the damn car.

"Yo, Rich. Wake up, man." I tapped Rich so we could go inside the crib. *Man, I know my mama about to be so happy to see me.*

"Where we at, man? I thought you was going home to Nat? And what the fuck happened to yo' hand?" I looked at my hand and it was bloody and swollen.

"Ain't shit happen, man. Come on, let's go inside. You drunk as shit." We hopped out the car and I went and grabbed the extra key my mom always keeps in the flowerpot. When I opened her door, her house smelled like fresh flowers. *Damn, this shit feels just like home. I guess this gonna be my home since my hoe of a wife fucked my brother.* I didn't know how, if or when I was going to tell mama about this shit. She was going to lose her fucking mind.

"I'm gonna crash on the couch, man."

"Naw, it's guest bedrooms down that hall. Mama don't like people sleeping on her couches and shit, especially in they outside clothes."

"Lil' mama's boy." Rich walked down the hall and went in one of the rooms, and I walked upstairs to find my mom. My mom didn't have a big mansion because she said she didn't want to live in a big ass house all alone. We got her this decent size five-bedroom house. She wanted a white picket fence and a garden in the front, so we helped out with that. My mom was a simple woman. Small things made her light with joy. When I made it to her room, I stood in the doorway and watched her and KJ peacefully sleeping. I didn't want to wake them, but I couldn't help it. I went over and tapped my mom on the shoulder. She jumped so hard I thought she was having a damn heart attack.

"Kaleef, baby, is that you?" She rubbed her eyes then opened them wider. "My God, it is you, baby!" She hopped up and gave me a big hug. We stood there rocking and hugging for at least five minutes. "How are you? Don't tell me you escaped prison?"

"Naw, I ain't escape, mama. They let me out because the prison was overcrowded. They let a lot of first time felons out."

"Why didn't you tell me to come get you?"

"I wanted to surprise y'all."

"Let me call your brothers. Oh, my goodness, prayer does work. Ain't God good, baby?" She grabbed her phone and started calling everybody she knew. I laid in the bed next to my son and pulled him in my arms. *This lil' nigga definitely my twin.* I tried to wake him but his little ass was not waking. It was almost five in the morning and my mom was on the phone inviting everyone over for a welcome home party for me. How I was feeling, I didn't want to be around nobody. I knew my mama wasn't going to let this shit pass though. She lived to throw parties.

"Ma, you know what time it is? Why you calling people, waking them up?"

"Oh, hush, boy. They ain't too sleep because everybody I'm calling is answering. Why in the hell isn't either of your brothers answering? Natalie is gonna be so happy. Have you talked to her yet?"

"Naw, ma." I lied because I wasn't ready to tell her what happened. I wanted her to throw this lil' party and then I'd tell her. I didn't need the whole family in my business, especially since I didn't fuck with them like that. None of my cousins wrote me or even came to visit. I was good on family. The only family I need was my mom and my son.

WHEN I OPENED MY EYES, the sun was shining in my face. My son wasn't next to me but I smelled my mama's cooking. *Damn, I missed the hell out of that smell.*

"Hey, baby, you finally woke." My mom walked in with a bunch of bags of clothes. "I sent Natalie to get you some clothes. I told her not to wake you because this is the first time you slept in a real bed in a long time. She's happy to see you, baby." *That bitch ain't happy to see shit but my brother's dick. Dick sucking ass bitch. Every chance I get I'm gonna disrespect that bitch.*

"I'm about to hop in the shower. I can hear people are starting to get here."

"Yeah, hurry up. Everyone is excited to see that handsome face of yours." I looked through the bags of clothes and I got pissed because the bitch knew me so damn well. She got everything she knew I would like. She even got me a Rolex watch. *That bitch knows I love watches.* And the watched was hella blinged out too.

"Cum dumpster ass bitch," I said to myself.

"So that's how you feel about your wife?" I turned to see Natalie standing in the doorway. She was looking good in her outfit, but in my eyes, at this moment, I saw her as a hoe on the street.

"Naw, bitch, that's how you feel about yourself. You better gon' on before I knock yo' ass out. Can't believe you did some shit like that to me. You couldn't find a random nigga to fuck? Naw, you had to go and open your legs for my fucking brother." I walked to her and wrapped my hands around neck. "Bitch, I should fucking kill you in here. And if you think you gonna act a fucking fool in front of my people guess again. We gonna go down here and act like we a happily married couple. I don't need them muthafuckas in my business." I let her ass go and pushed her out the room. I headed to the bathroom so I could get ready and get this day over with.

Walking down the stairs, I could see everybody chilling and laughing and shit. If I wasn't so pissed, I would be happy to see my family.

"Daddyyyyyyyyyy." To see my son run to me, calling me daddy, warmed my heart. *He's so young and innocent.* I picked him up gave him a high five.

"What's up, lil' man? You happy to see daddy?"

"Yes, daddy. Can I play with yo' phone? Mommy left my tablet at home."

"Yeah, you can see my phone. You gotta show me how to work it though."

"Ok."

"Brooooo! What's up, man? I thought mama was lying." Kanan walked up and pulled me in for a brotherly hug. Man, I was happy as hell to see my lil' bro.

"What's up, lil nigga? Damn, you all grown and shit now. Look at you. Nigga, I raised yo' lil' ass."

"Man, cut all that out. Come on, man. Lib out here on the spade table." I followed him to the backyard where most of the family was. Everyone started clapping and hugging me and shit. I felt loved, even if most of their asses were phony. I still felt the love from my family.

When I laid eyes on Kalib, I wanted to beat his ass again. He didn't look hurt. That lil' nigga was balled up, protecting his face when I beat his ass. That was why he was looking normal.

"What's up, lil bro? Stand up and give me a hug." Kalib looked scared as shit, but he got his ass up. I grabbed his hand, squeezed it hard as fuck, and pulled him into me. "I ain't say shit so you don't say shit." He snatched away from me and sat back down.

"Glad to have you home, big brother," Kalib said with a sly grin on his face.

"Alright, everybody, it's time to eat." When my mom said that, everyone got up and went to sit at the long picnic table she has in her backyard. Only God knew how long I'd been wanting my mama's cooking. Natalie tried to go sit by Kalib, but I snatched her ass up. Thank God nobody was paying attention.

"Bitch, I will embarrass you out here," I whispered in her ear. I didn't know why the fuck she was mad at me. I was the one that caught her fucking my damn brother.

"You gonna act childish all day?" Natalie asked while taking a seat.

"You gonna act whorish all day?" Shut her ass right on up.

TWENTY-ONE

Aniya

"I'm living my best life! It's my birthday, least that's what I'm dressed like!" I was singing my heart out to Cardi B and Chance the Rapper's song "Best Life". "But she trapping and she had to make it happen for her life. Don't be mad 'cause she having shit, you had it your whole life!" Every time that part came on I snapped because I felt it in my soul! I worked hard to make it where I was at and I was damn proud.

"I made a couple Ms with my best friend! Turned all my Ls into lessons!" Drea sang along with me. We both were feeling good off the shots of Hennessy and Patron. It was raining shots as soon as we stepped in the club.

"That's right, cousin! Turn the fuck up! You deserve it, bitchhh!" Drea bent over, twerking all over me. I just slapped her ass and made it rain ones, fives, and twenties.

"Ayyye!"

"Bitch, you know this ain't a strip joint, right?"

"Girl, I don't give a damn! I'm happy as fuck! I got my fav with me, I'm single, and feeling good! You better take this free money, girl!"

Drea fell in the booth laughing hysterically. "I swear yo' ass is tore up! Girl, you know you ain't single!"

"Who my man? Where he at?" I placed my hands on my thick and wide hips. I was feeling so good today, and I went out and splurged at the mall. Me and Drea did. "Matter of fact, let's go to the dance floor!"

I pulled Drea up before she could protest. Usually, she was the one who had to get me to turn up. Tonight the roles were reversed. I noticed she wasn't as into it like she usually was. I knew for a fact that she was missing Kanan. She'd swear it was fuck him, but I knew better. That was why I invited him out tonight. I wanted to share this day with everybody who was special to me. I couldn't pay my mama to step foot into the club. She said she had something real special planned for me though.

Over the past few months, Kanan became like the big brother I never had. He was always nice to me and protective. He swore he'd fight any nigga that looked my way. At first, I thought he was only doing it because of his brother. I soon found out there were no opportunistic intentions involved.

I also appreciated him for all the times he was cool with me going out with him and Drea. I knew if it was me, I would've been annoyed. He never showed it or voiced it to me, and for that, I was grateful.

Two songs had played and I was ready to sit down. These heels were starting to hurt. Tonight I was wearing a peach, two piece short set. The shirt was a crop top that only covered my boobs. It had a small V in the middle so my cleavage was out there. The shorts were high waisted so only a portion of my stomach was showing. The only thing about the shorts was they appeared snug and a little skimpy on me. It was only because my ass and hips. I loved the way I looked though, so that was all that mattered.

Walking off the dance floor, I stepped out of the six-inch nude

Giuseppes. They were bad with a gold strap and I accessorized with gold jewelry to make my ensemble pop. I was looking good, smelling good, and feeling better.

On cue, the DJ was playing "Best Life" again. This was his third time playing it and I was loving it. "I'm living my best life! It's my birthday, at least that's what I'm dressed like!"

"You dressed like you about to get a nigga killed for staring at you in these little ass clothes." Kanan's voice vibrated in my ear. I quickly stood and tried to straighten my clothes as much as I could. I felt like a little sister getting caught in the club by her big brother.

"Naw, don't try and hide now. You living yo' best life, huh?" Kanan mean mugged me. I started to feel ashamed, like I was doing something bad. He cracked a smile then a laugh. "You know I'm just playing with you, sis. Where my wife? I know her ass in here acting up too."

I looked behind me because that was where I last saw her. She was just there. "I don't know. Maybe she saw you come in and got scared."

"Haha, that ain't funny, sis. I'm for real."

"I really don't know, K. She was just right there until you came." I pointed on the dance floor where Drea was dancing before. Kanan studied me for some seconds before shaking his head and laughing.

"Sis, yo' ass lit up. Where y'all section? Come on."

Leading the way, I practiced walking straight so I wouldn't fall. I was starting to feel heavy, like I was about to fall. "K, you go find Drea. I'm going to chill here 'til y'all come back, okay?"

"Aight, drunk ass. Stay. Right. Here." He made himself clear. I nodded and waved him off. I wasn't going no damn where, unless I was being carried out. That was how heavy these drinks had me feeling.

"We got to stop meeting like this, mama." I heard a deep and sexy voice say. It reminded me so much of Kalib's my head snapped in the direction it was coming from.

Just like that, my mood shifted to me being annoyed. "Ain't nobody meet your no driving ass nowhere. You must be stalking me."

"Shawty, I ain't never had to stalk no bitch. Ain't about to start doing the shit now." He came and sat in my section, helping himself to my liquor. He poured two shots. I assumed one was for me and one for him. Nope, he took both of them to the head.

I kissed my teeth loudly in annoyance. "Ugh, I didn't invite you to sit next to me. Nor did I say it was okay to drink off my bottle."

"I ain't have to ask to sit next to you. This a free fucking country." He poured himself another drink. *This nigga real rude and disrespectful.* I was mad at myself for getting so twisted I couldn't move. That didn't stop me from running my mouth though.

"Free fucking country my ass. Nigga, you need to get out my section." I pushed myself up as best I could. I caught a glimpse at my feet and noticed they were a little swollen. They were also sore. The guy looked down at my feet and scoffed.

"How you bossing niggas around like you own the joint? As I said, this a free country. I want to sit here. Deal with it or bounce." He simply shrugged, like this was section to begin with. "From the looks of it, yo' ass stuck with them little swollen ass feet."

I sat there glaring at him, not knowing what to say next. I wanted to get up and fight this rude ass nigga. Lord knew that wasn't happening though. *Ugh, Niya! Who told your ass to get this drunk?!*

"Fix your face, shawty. You looking constipated. You need me to help your cute ass to the bathroom?" he offered in a sincere tone. That threw me off a little as I stared him in the face.

I ain't going to lie, this nigga was *fione!* He had smooth milk chocolate skin that made me want to lick him to see how he tasted. He had the sexiest, fullest pair of pink lips. *Damn, I want to bite his lips too.* I was also loving the way his hairline was tapered and faded just right. His wild and scruffy beard turned me on. He put me in the mind of a sexy and chiseled caveman. He had on an all-black, long sleeved shirt but I could see his muscles bulging on his arms. I was now imaging him without a shirt. *Damn.*

Snap! Snap! Snap!

"Aye, shawty! You can stop undressing me with your eyes now." He called me out.

"Huh? Nigga, you wish I was checking for your ass." I popped an attitude.

Suddenly, I smelled weed. The smell was so strong I knew I was catching a high. I then noticed he had a lit blunt between his thumb and index finger.

"You want some?" He held the blunt close enough to my lips. The smoke seeping from it got in my mouth and I went into a coughing fit. I wasn't a weed smoker so I knew for a fact I was light weight.

"I'm gon' report your ass trying to give me asthma!" I slapped him in the shoulder. "Ow, shit!"

"You shouldn't be putting your hands where they don't belong."

"Fuck you. You shouldn't be sitting where you don't belong." I rolled my eyes at his ass.

"I can fuck you if that's what you want. I told you before I can sit where I want. You should be sitting in my lap." This nigga didn't warn me or let me make the choice. He just picked me up like I was light as a feather and placed me on his lap. My eyes got big and I stiffened when I felt his third leg resting right between my legs through his jeans.

I tried to move but he had a firm hold on me. "Where you going? This what you wanted."

"Sir, please let me go before I scream."

"As long as you're screaming my name, we good."

"Ugh! Do you always say the first thing you think?"

"Are you always a bitch?"

"Nigga, you—"

"Kaleef? Is that you?" Some woman passing our section stopped to talk to him. *Hmm, Kaleef...I like that.*

"Stephanie, what's up?" He nodded, holding onto me tighter. I tried to move so he could talk but he had a good grip on me. "Aye, shawty, stay your ass right here. This where you belong."

My words were now stuck in my throat. This was the first time since he came over to my section I was at a loss for words.

"Umm, where is my soror?" Stephanie turned her nose up at me and rolled her eyes. *This bitch doesn't know me to be rolling her beady ass eyes.*

"Not here. Anything else?" Kaleef shrugged her off in a nonchalant demeanor. I thought he was being rude with me. He was really treating the chick like she was nothing.

"No, have a good night." She walked away quickly with a smile. Her smile was about as real as a two-dollar bill.

I heard her say soror so now I was wondering if this nigga had a girl. If he did, I didn't want to be in his lap.

"Kaleef, I need to get up and find my cousin." I was trying to pry his hands off me, but that wasn't doing anything. His only moved from my waist, to my thighs, and now he had a handful of my ass. He gave it a gentle squeeze and stared intensely into my eyes.

"I'm going to let you get up but come back to me. Don't have me looking all over this club for that ass. If I find it in the wrong hands, I'm going to show my ass. Neither of us want that."

I stared at him crazy. I so badly wanted to go off and say a bunch of shit, but I thought of the outcome and decided to just get up and nod. "Ok."

After checking the dance floor and the bar, I still couldn't find Kanan or Drea. Heading to the bathroom, I had to pee anyway. I was also praying I found Drea in here.

"Excuse you," I said when a chick bumped into me. She quickly turned around and got into my face.

"No, bitch, excuse you. You think you can bring your hoe ass into this club and steal another woman's man? Huh, whore?"

Blankly, I stared at her. Her lines sounded so rehearsed I couldn't believe she was being serious. "Girl, get out my face." I shoved past her.

The next thing I knew she had me by the hair and was pulling me back. "Umm no, I'm not finished talking—aghhh!"

I turned around and two pieced her ass so fast she didn't see it coming. I might've been quiet and kept to myself when I was younger but best believe I could hold my own. Too many hoes in the hood used to try me until they found out.

Ole girl came charging towards me like a bull. I just stood there and waited for her to come closer. When she did, I ran her nose right into my fist. "Aggghh, my nose!"

There was blood pouring out her nose and to the floor. I laughed as I watched her cry about her nose. The shit was probably fake. While she was crying, I left the bathroom. I remembered there being another bathroom in this club. It was so big, there should be at least three.

"Ahhh, Kanan! Fuck meee, ba-a-abyy!"

"Shit, Drea! You been giving my pussy away?"

"Nooo, daddy, it's yours! Allll yours!"

"Y'all some nasty niggas!" I yelled at K and Drea. They ignored me and continued to fuck.

I had to pee so bad I used the stall two doors down and left the bathroom. I was ready to go and they were in the bathroom fucking. Was it weird that I was horny now? I hadn't had sex in years. The closest thing I got to it was Kalib giving me head.

Damn, it's been almost a month since we talked. I miss him so much. Drea kept telling me to just call him. I was stubborn when it came to stuff like that. Right now, I really wanted him. I just wanted to kiss him and feel him and be in his strong arms.

"Lord, please help me." I prayed before dialing Kalib's phone. There were a few rings until he picked up and requested to Face-Time. At least, I thought it was him.

"Yes?" It was none other than Natalie.

"Um, where is Kalib and why are you answering his phone?"

"Kalib is busy at the moment. What do *you* want?"

"I want to speak to my man, bitch!"

"No, girl, you mean *our* man." She snickered.

"Nata—"

"Aye, ma, somebody call while I was in the shower?"

"No, baby!" Was the last thing I heard before the phone disconnected.

TWENTY-TWO

Andrea

It was the morning after Aniya's party and I just wished I could sleep in some more. Kanan had some of his homeboys over playing the game. You would think since he lived in a mansion his house would be soundproof. Being back with Kanan had been great. He apologized for acting like a fool and I accepted his apology. At the end of the day, I knew I couldn't stay away from that man. I fell in love, and that was something I never expected to happen. I just wanted to be happy with him without any distractions. That was why I put Darius' ass on the block list and I had private calls blocked as well. I didn't even answer my phone for anybody except my aunt, my cousin, and Kanan. Darius could find another fish to fry. I wasn't giving up any information on my man.

"Hello." I answered my phone for Aniya. Her ass called me every morning talking about nothing.

"Girl, stop acting like you sleep. I have to tell you what happened last night before you and Kanan snuck off to do the nasty."

"What happened, bitch?" She gave me the whole run down of her and the guy that hit my damn truck. She even told me about Natalie answering Kalib's phone. The shit pissed me off so bad because I told her to watch out for that bitch Natalie. Kalib was a dirty dog. What kind of dude hooked up with his brother's wife? All the good I saw in Kalib quickly faded. "Girl, fuck Kalib's nasty ass. That's some *Flowers in the Attic* type of shit. Stay away from his ass."

"Girl, you ain't gotta tell me. I'm just glad I never let him hit. He tasted it a couple of times but that's it."

"So about this new guy. Are you gonna call or text him?"

"Girl, I don't know. He's too damn aggressive and demanding for me. You know I like to call the shots. He's so fucking sexy though. I can't get that handsome face out of my mind."

"Girl, look at you. You don't waste no time moving on, huh?"

"I'm over Kalib. I ain't got time for that shit."

"Girl, you should hear these niggas downstairs playing the game. They acting like they really in the NBA, and I'm about to go cuss they asses out." I got up from the bed and grabbed my silk, pink robe that went all the way down to my ankles. I put my weave up in a messy bun and slipped on my Nike slides.

"Hello!" Aniya yelled through the phone.

"Yeah, girl, I'm about go cuss them out. You can stay on the phone. This ain't gonna take long."

"Girl, you funny as hell. That man gonna put you out his crib."

"I wish his ass would." I ran down the long ass staircase and walked into the living room. It was only Kanan and two other guys so I didn't understand why the hell they were so damn loud. They didn't see me standing behind them because they kept talking shit to each other. "Why the fuck y'all gotta be so damn loud in here?" I screamed as loud as I could so they could see how I was feeling. They all jumped and turned to look at me. When I saw that two guys were the ones that hit my car, I almost fainted. It was the guy that Aniya was swooning over. *Why the fuck is he here?*

"Damn, bae, you just scared the shit out of us." Kanan stood up and came to give me a hug and kiss but my eyes were still on his company.

"Aye, ma, don't I know you?" Dude asked me.

"You're the dude that hit my car."

"What? Kaleef is over there?" Aniya screamed through the phone.

"You the drunk no driving nigga that hit my baby truck?" Kanan started cracking up laughing.

"Who is he, K?"

"Baby, this my big brother Kaleef. Remember I told you he just got out?"

"Your brother?"

"His brother?" Aniya yelled through the phone again.

"Niya, I'm gonna call you back."

"Nooooo, bitch, don't ha—" I hung up on her ass. This shit was starting to feel like the twilight zone. A bitch needed answers.

"So you're Natalie's husband, right?"

"Yup." He sounded disappointed when he answered that question.

"Ummm, ok. Maybe we should all go out since Kalib and Aniya are dating." I wanted to test him to see how he would react to me saying that because I knew he knew exactly who Aniya was.

"Aw, word? They fucking around?" Kaleef asked while breaking out in laughter.

"Wait, I thought they broke up?" Kanan's dumb ass was standing beside me looking dumbfounded and confused.

"If not, then they will be," Kaleef said while taking a seat.

"What?" Kanan was still acting dumb as shit.

"Shut up, Kanan." I stormed off toward the kitchen so I could call my cousin back.

"Aye, girl, you better watch yo' damn mouth."

"Yeah, whatever." I yelled over my shoulder. It was some crazy shit going on. I wondered if Kaleef knew about his hoe wife and his disloyal brother. *The way he was talking he has to know something.*

"KANAN, you can't keep coming through my damn work phone like this," I silently yelled at him for the hundredth time today. He'd been calling back to back, talking about he couldn't find this and where is that.

"If you ain't rearrange all my shit, I would be able to find shit! Always touching shit, girl, damn. Where is all my damn cologne?"

"Your cologne is on the dresser. Why would you have it on the bathroom sink? That's just dumb."

"Stop touching my shit. Drea. I'm not playing, girl."

"Well where am I supposed to put my shit, K?"

"All these rooms in this house. Pick one and stop rearranging my room." I was about to say something else but his ass hung up on me. Lately, I'd been living with Kanan because we hated being apart. I had so much shit at his house I needed to rearrange a few things and his room was set up so wrong it irritated me. Who puts all the linen in their room closet? The linen was supposed to be in a hall closet.

"Ugh, he gets on my damn nerves," I said aloud to myself. I stood up because I was ready to go on my damn lunch break. I'd been here five hours and I hadn't ate shit yet. *Lord knows I'm starving.* I headed right out the door, not even bothering to ask Aniya if she wanted anything because she said she brought leftovers my aunt cooked. When I got to the parking lot, I noticed I was smiling from ear to ear. I guessed that was what happened when you were in a happy relationship. As soon as I made it to my car, someone grabbed me by my hair and slammed me against the door. When I finally got the chance to open my eyes, I saw it was Darius.

"Bitch, you really thought I wasn't gonna get up with you?" He had me hemmed against the door so I couldn't move.

"Let me the fuck go."

"Bitch, you must really want to go to jail for the rest of yo' life. You really love that nigga, huh?"

"You damn right, and I ain't telling you shit or setting him up so give that folder to whoever the fuck you want!" He began choking me so I started swinging on his ass.

Click, clack!

We both froze when we heard a gun load up. I was happy and relieved to see it was Kaleef.

Get yo' muthafucking hands off her, nigga." Darius let me go and ran off like the little bitch that he was. "You good? What the fuck was that about? You lucky I was riding past and spotted yo' lil' ass. That's yo' other nigga or something? You know I gotta run this shit by my brother."

"No, please don't!"

"And why shouldn't I? You out here playing him and shit."

"I'm not playing him. I wouldn't do that to him. I love Kanan."

"Well tell me what that shit was about." Kaleef was dead set on knowing why Darius was roughing me up. I had to tell him or he would tell Kanan something that wasn't true. I told him to get in my truck so I could tell him the whole story. After I told him how Darius was blackmailing me to get to his brothers, he was pissed.

"So why you ain't tell my brother?"

"I didn't want him to know about my past. It's embarrassing and I didn't want him to think I was using him. Our whole relationship I haven't asked that man for shit. I still work and I buy shit for his home. I just want to be with him in peace."

"I feel all that, but you still should have told him. Either way, he still gonna be pissed. I'm gonna see what I can do about this bitch ass nigga though."

"I can handle myself, Kaleef."

"I ain't doing this for you. That nigga trying to come at my family, and I ain't letting that shit fly."

"I thought the McClain brothers didn't get their hands dirty?"

"They don't, but I do. I'll see you around, shawty. Be safe out here." I let out I sigh of relief knowing Kaleef would handle Darius. I knew he was still going to tell Kanan what happened, but I guessed that was what the hell I got for not saying shit in the first place. I decided to go home for the rest of the day because I was pretty sure that bitch ass nigga bruised my neck up. I needed to check my mail anyway because I hadn't been there in a while.

TWENTY-THREE

Kanan

After my brother told me about Drea and that bitch ass nigga Darius, I was livid. *How could she not tell me what was going on? Did she really plan on setting me up?* So many thoughts ran through my mind as I sat at my kitchen island. Drea had the nerve not to come home yesterday. She knew exactly what she was doing. She knew I was going to go hard on her ass. I'd been texting her all morning, telling her to bring her ass back. She'd been taking her sweet ass time though.

When I heard the door open, I hopped from the kitchen island and met her ass in the foyer. She was standing there with her arms folded and a nasty look on her face. She was acting like she was ready for war. *She's the one that's always doing dumb shit then tries to flip shit on me.*

"I don't know what the fuck you standing there looking ugly for. I should knock you the fuck out." I jumped at her but her ass didn't flinch. "Aw, you think you tough, huh? Bring yo' ass in here and sit down, man." I walked into the living room and she followed behind me. I pushed her ass down on the couch and I sat on the coffee table so I could look her in her eyes. "So you tried to set me up, huh?"

"No, you know I wouldn't do that."

"That's what I thought, but you could have been playing me this whole damn time. You should have came to me, and I would've helped you. You don't think I'm man enough to take care of you?"

"That's not it, Kanan. I just didn't want you to know about my past."

"I already knew about yo' fucking past. You think I would let you in my crib if I ain't trust you? I already had a background check and all that shit did on you. I'm not stupid, I know what bitches want from me. I'm rich as shit and bitches tend to fuck with me for my money. I love yo' ass, girl, but you sit up here and bring more problems to the fucking relationship. Now I gotta go clean this shit up." I stood up and went walking toward the door.

"Where you going, Kanan?" She followed behind me and started grabbing the back of my shirt.

"You better stop putting yo' hands on me before I knock yo' ass out."

"I said where the fuck you going?"

"I gotta handle some business."

"Don't kill that man, Kanan."

"Do I look like a killer to you? Yo, get the fuck out my face. And don't leave this fucking house."

"When you coming back?"

"I don't know. Just keep yo' ass here until I say it's cool for you to leave."

"Kanan, please!" She had tears streaming down her face, looking all ugly and shit. I wanted to laugh but now wasn't the time.

"Man, gone on in the house and don't leave." I hopped in my car and sped off. I had plans on following Kaleef and Rich to wherever they were trying to find Darius. Kaleef usually didn't get his hands dirty so I knew Rich would probably handle Darius. I knew Kaleef would most likely leave his crib when it got dark so I planned on hiding out in front of his crib and following them. I just needed to see that nigga's face. I needed to let him know I wasn't to be fucked with. He fucked with the wrong McClain brother. As soon as I was about to pull in front of Kaleef's crib, my phone rang.

"Yooo."

"Aye, bro, I need a big favor from you."

"What's up, Kalib? I'm busy right now, man."

"Well you gonna have to stop whatever you doing and get to the dealership. I need you to take this Lamborghini to Trev." Trev was one of our highest paying customers. Whatever he wanted, we gave it to him with no questions asked. We didn't even know that nigga's real name. That was how rich the nigga was. We never fucked up a delivery when it came to Trev.

"Why you can't do it?" I needed to know what was so important that he couldn't take Trev the car since he was the only one that did transport.

"New shipment coming and they need me to sign for it. We can't miss this shipment and Trev needs that car ASAP."

"That's a two hour drive, man."

"So? It's gonna already be somebody there to bring you back."

"Aight, man, I'm on my way." If I hurried, I could be back before night fall and still follow Kaleef and Rich to wherever the hell Darius was hiding. When I got to the dealership, the car was already in the back, ready to go.

"Aye, bro, don't fuck this up. You ain't did a drop off in a minute. I know I can trust you with this."

"I got it, bro, damn." He threw me the keys and I hopped in. *I'm gonna have to get one of these. This muthafucka drive real smooth.* My thoughts went to my girl. I was so pissed at her but that girl made me happy every damn day. I turned the music up loud so I could chill and make the ride comfortable. I pushed my foot harder on the gas so I could see how fast the car went. It was definitely fast as shit. I nodded my head to the music while driving down the empty road. I was shocked that I was damn near the only person on the road.

I looked in my rearview mirror and noticed a black Jeep behind me. The truck was kind of on my ass so I sped up a bit. When I sped up, so did the truck. *I know this nigga ain't following me.* I started going ninety miles per hour. *Yup, this bitch ass nigga following me. Why though?* I put the pedal to the metal and hoped I would lose his ass but he was right on my ass. I tried to grab my phone so I could call somebody but the phone fell to the floor. When I looked up... *Bam!*

I hit a fucking tree.

TWENTY-FOUR

Aniya

Kaleef and Kalib are brothers. *Kaleef and Kalib are brothers?*
Kaleef and Kalib are brothers! That had been running
through my mind all day while I was at work. I couldn't get over it.
How did I get mixed up in something like this? Me and Kalib had
dated but I was now attracted to Kaleef. *Am I wrong?* Would I be a
hoe for thinking about Kaleef in ways I shouldn't be thinking of a
married man? *Kaleef is married to Natalie!*

"Huuuuh!" I dramatically gasped and shook my head. I had to
rub my temple to get my thoughts together. I didn't know why I was
so worried about Kaleef and Kalib anyway. They were both non-
factors to me.

"Aniya?" Ben walked into my office without knocking. I hated
when he did that shit. Still, I always kept a smile.

"Hey, Ben. What can I do for you?"

He took a seat in front of my desk, adjusted his black tie, and
cleared his throat. *Oh, boy. What is it now?* He always did this when

he wanted me to do something. It was either he wanted me to fire somebody or to cover a shift.

"We have a problem."

I lightly chuckled. "*We* have a problem? Or *you* have a problem?"

"*We* as in the *company* has a problem." He crossed his legs and interlocked his fingers.

"And what would that be, Ben?"

"Well...let me tell you a story, Niya."

Niya? Nigga, you don't know me like that! "Mhm, okay." I nodded with the same smile that never left my face.

"There comes a time when we have to move on, you know? We have to do something new. Things don't fit anymore so they're out of place. So we have to fix them. You get what I'm saying?" He was up and walking around my office. It wasn't too big or too small. It was actually a little bigger than Ben's. I knew for a fact he was mad about it when I got my promotion. His position was higher than mines, but he had a smaller office.

"Yes, I know exactly what you're saying." I exhaled. I knew this nigga wanted me to do something. "You want me to fire someone?"

"No, that's not it." He solemnly shook his head.

"Then what is it?" My heartbeat sped and felt like it was now beating outside my chest.

"As you know, our sensors have been extremely low lately. Cooperate wants to make some budget cuts, starting with payroll." He stopped talking to stare at me over the rims of his glasses. My stomach began to flip flop and I suddenly had to use the bathroom.

"Okay, so what are you saying, Ben?" Even though I feared asking that question, I had to know.

"I'm saying that, umm...it saddens me to say this but—"

"Dammit, Ben, spit the shit out already!" I barked. I wasn't trying to be rude at first, but he was pissing me off by beating around the bush.

"We have to let you, along with two handfuls of people go, Aniya. I'm sorry."

"So, you came in here to fire me..." I slowly nodded. As I blankly stared off into space, I felt my eye twitch. *I just celebrated my anniversary of being here for six years and now this nigga is firing me?*

"I'm not just firing you. One hundred other employees are getting laid off as well."

"What about you, Ben? You getting laid off too?"

"Well, I um—"

"That's what the fuck I thought!" I slapped my hand on my desk. "You know how long I waited to get in the position I'm in now? You know how much work I put in? I did your job, my job, and everybody else's up in here! Y'all can't just fire me!"

"Aniya, this wasn't in my ha—"

"Oh, bullshit, it wasn't! I bet you couldn't wait to get me out of here so you can have my office. You know what? You can have it! You can kiss my ass too, ole bald head, dirty, nerdy, Uncle Tom, ass kissing bitch!"

"Aniya, I'm appalled at your—"

"Oh, fuck you, Ben!" I was snatching and shoving all my belongings into my work bag. I didn't have much in my office. Just a family picture of my cousin and mama and a mug I never used filled with pens.

"And, bitch, what the fuck your ass staring at?" I snapped at Brandy's nosey ass on the way out. She was always in somebody else's business. She knew all the tea about everybody at the job. I was surprised nobody here had beat her ass.

"Aniya! Aniya! Aniya!" Ben continued to yell my name on the way out the office. I wasn't stopping for his ass. I was for real when I said fuck him!

As soon as I was safely inside my car, I broke down crying. I didn't want to, but I couldn't help it. *How could they fire me?* I put so much into that stupid company. I worked my ass off every day to standout just to get fired?

What was I supposed to tell my mama and cousin? We all paid rent in our apartment. *God, what am I supposed to do now?*

I went around the corner to this milkshake shack I loved. I just needed to calm down and figure out my next move in life. I'd thought I found something I was good at. *Guess I was dead ass wrong.*

"Hey, ma, what you doing in here all by yourself?" I heard that deep, sexy voice and I creamed in my pants a little. I turned around and there Kaleef was, standing right behind me.

"Ok, now I really think you're a stalker," I said while turning around in my stool and sipping my milkshake.

"Naw, I was just walking past with my lil' homie and I saw you in here looking sad. Thought I would come and cheer you up."

"You know I dated your brother, right?"

"So! Did he hit?"

"Hell naw!"

"So that shit don't count. If he did hit, I still wouldn't care. He ain't care what he did to me." I could tell he was venting without trying to.

"What you mean by that? What did he do to you?" I wanted to see if he knew what I knew.

"He fucked my wife. He can have that rat ass hoe. Aye, don't tell nobody what I just told you."

"Yo' secret's safe with me. So are you trying to mess with me to get back at yo' brother? I don't play those type of games."

"I was flirting with you before I knew you even had history with my brother so what that tell you, shawty?" He was looking at me so intensely. It was like he was trying to read my soul and eat my face off at the same damn time. His smell was so intoxicating. It was like he was putting a spell on me. He leaned in for a kiss and I met him half-way. Like I said, it was like he put a spell on me to do whatever he wanted to me. He grabbed the back of my neck and stuck his tongue down my throat. I moaned inside of his mouth as he sucked on my tongue. He broke our kiss once his phone rang.

"What you want, nigga? What? Alright, I'm on my way."

"Everything ok?" I felt the need to ask him.

"Naw, Kanan got in a car accident. I gotta go."

"Oh, my god, Andrea! I'm coming too." He grabbed my hand and we rushed to his car. When we got to the emergency room, we walked in hand and hand and went ran right into Kalib. He looked down at our hands and I knew he was pissed.

"What the fuck is this?" He asked us. I was quiet as a damn church mouse. I ain't owe him an explanation for shit. Not right now, not this time at least.

"Go sit down," Kaleef told me in that sexy, demanding voice. And I did exactly what he said.

TWENTY-FIVE

Kaleef

When I got the call about my little brother being in a car accident, I stopped everything and rushed to the emergency room. I was in the middle of going to find that bitch ass nigga Darius, but I ended up bumping into Aniya's sexy ass. Kalib was the one who called and said I needed to get to the emergency room. I wasn't even gonna answer my phone when his name popped up but thank God I did. When Aniya and I walked in the emergency room, Kalib was pissed. He wanted answers but I ain't say shit to him. We were waiting in the emergency room on opposite sides of the room. Andrea had been pacing the floor back and forth since we'd arrived.

"Come on, sis, come sit down. You worrying yourself," Kalib told Andrea.

"Man, leave her alone. That's her man in there fighting for his life," I said while giving him a dirty look.

"Man, now ain't the time to be acting petty. Our brother in the fucking hospital," Kalib said while shaking his head. He was right, but every and any time I had the time to be petty with him I was going to do it. He was my brother so I couldn't kill him, but I could hate him for what he did to me.

"Where's my damn baby?" My mom screamed while running toward us. "What happened to him?"

"He was in a car accident." Andrea answered.

"Who the hell are you?" My mom asked with her nose turned up at Andrea.

"I'm his girlfriend."

"My son doesn't have a girlfriend because if he did I would have met her. Now excuse me, I need to see what's going on with my child." My mom bumped past her and went to the front desk. Yeah, our mom was that kind of mom. She wasn't approving of no woman. No one was good enough for her boys. It took her years to accept Natalie. After we got married, she had no choice. Now her and Natalie were cool as shit. That was why I hadn't told her or anyone what happened between her and Kalib.

"Come on, they said we can go see him now," my mom said while leading us to his room. Aniya decided to stay in the waiting room. When we got to his room, he was laid there with his eyes closed. Andrea ran to his right side and my mom ran to his left side. He opened his eyes and smiled.

"Baby, you ok?" Andrea and my mom asked in unison. My mom gave her an ugly look and I couldn't help but laugh a little.

"Ma, this my girlfriend, Andrea. I ain't get a chance to bring her to meet you yet. I'm sorry y'all gotta meet like this," Kanan said in whispers.

"Don't worry about that. Just rest your voice, honey," my mom said while fluffing his pillows.

"Bro, what happened? I know you wasn't drinking again while delivering the car?" Kalib had the nerve to ask.

"I wasn't drinking, man. You saw me when I picked up the car. I think somebody was following, trying to run me off the road or something." Andrea looked at me and I knew we were thinking the same thing. It had to be Darius.

"Man, you know we lost our biggest client because of this?" Kalib yelled.

"Fuck that client! Our lil' brother is laying here hurt and all you thinking about is a fucking client?" I yelled while jumping his in face.

"Man, you better gone on, Kaleef. Our business ain't got shit to do with you. You been gone for years. I been holding these dealerships down with little help from him and no help from you."

"Bitch ass nigga, I will drop you where you stand." Kalib knew better then to play these games with me so I didn't know why he even tried it.

"Hey, y'all stop all of the mess while my baby is here in this bed. Kalib, apologize to your brothers now!" my mom yelled, but Kalib ain't have the balls to apologize. He thought he was better than us because he put more work into the companies. To be honest, I didn't give a fuck about those damn companies. I was getting my portion either way. My father left each of us money that would last a lifetime. If he thought I gave a fuck about a dealership, he was dead wrong.

The door swung opened and it seemed like my eyes were deceiving me. It was Dawn. Dawn was Kanan's first love. I hadn't seen her since before I got locked up. Dawn liked to travel the world. She'd been some of everywhere. The last time she decided to leave Kanan told her to never come back. He was tired of her leaving him so he vowed to never, ever take her back. He said that every time she left but soon as she came back he accepted her each time. I was guessing she'd been to Paris because she stood dressed in a trench coat, sunglasses, and a hat.

You could tell Kanan hadn't seen her in a while because he was sitting there speechless with glossy eyes.

"Dawn, baby, I'm glad you made it." My mom went to give her a big hug. My mom loved Dawn. She always said Dawn should have been her daughter-in-law.

"You invited her here, ma?" Kanan asked.

"Yeah, she called me last night and said she would be in town.

When I got the call that you were in here, I thought she would want to see you."

"Am I missing something?" Andrea asked. I was done. I didn't want to see the results so I stormed out the room. All this shit was a damn soap opera. When I turned the corner, I bumped into someone. I didn't see who. I just saw papers and an ultrasound. I picked up the papers and stood to hand them to the lady.

"I'm sorry, miss. Here go yo' papers." When I looked up, it was Natalie. I looked back down at the ultrasound sound and the pregnancy papers and smoke started coming out of my ears. I hadn't had sex with her at all since my release so it meant this bitch is pregnant by my brother or someone else. I dropped the papers and wrapped my hands around her neck. It was like I blacked out. All I heard was people screaming and seeing Natalie fall to the floor. *Damn, what the fuck did I just do?*

To be Continued

Bless Our Page With A LIKE!

Make Sure To Join Our Reader's Group!
Join Here!

Grab Our Upcoming Releases!
Check Out Our Releases!